Ace's Heart

An Ex-Mafia, Second Chance, Christian Romance

Abiegail Rose

Staten House

Staten House

Editing & Layout by Abiegail Rose

Book Cover by Abiegail Rose

Dear Readers

I hope this letter finds you well. It is with great joy and a heart full of purpose that I share this news with you. As some of you may know, I have been writing under the pen name Abiegail Rose, weaving tales of passion, desire, and love in the pages of spicy romance novels. But today, I stand at a crossroads—a moment of transformation and revelation.

Why the shift? The answer lies in my journey—a journey that has led me to a deeper understanding of faith, grace, and the boundless love of our Lord. Recently my life has had many changed: I graduated with a Bachelors in Religious Studies, I got married, and I finally found a nurturing church home—through all of the trails, growing, and learning, my heart was stirred. The more I grew closer to the Lord, the more I realized that my purpose as a writer needed to align with my newfound convictions.

The Calling: It was as if a divine whisper echoed through my soul. I felt called to dedicate everything I do to the Lord—to honor Him with my words, my stories, and my creativity. And so, with unwavering resolve, I am embarking on a new literary path—one that reflects the purity of heart, the beauty of redemption, and the strength of love rooted in faith.

Norman, My Anchor: My husband, Norman, has been my steadfast companion on this journey. His unwavering support, his prayers, and his encouragement have fortified my resolve. Together, we believe that these novels—rooted in faith and love—will touch hearts, uplift spirits, and bring hope to those who seek solace in the written word.

A Safe Harbor: My promise to you, dear readers, is this: These novels will be a safe harbor—a place where you can immerse yourself in love stories without fear of temptation, where passion is tempered by virtue, and where the light of Christ shines brightly. Whether you read them by the fireplace, on a park bench, or during your morning commute, know that these pages are infused with prayers, grace, and the promise of redemption.

Thank You: Thank you for joining me on this pilgrimage. May my words resonate with your soul, and may you find joy, inspiration, and a renewed sense of hope within these stories. Let us embark on this adventure together, hand in hand, guided by faith and fueled by love.

With gratitude and anticipation,

Abiegail Rose

"I DON'T NEED A KNIGHT IN SHINING ARMOR, I NEED A WARRIOR CLAD IN THE FULL ARMOR OF GOD"

Harmonies of Havencrest

PROLOGUE

Melanie Barnett stood at the front of the church; the choir arrayed behind her like a tapestry of voices waiting to be woven into song. The morning light streamed through the stained-glass windows, casting a celestial glow over the scene. She closed her eyes for a moment, a silent prayer on her lips. "Lord, fill me up," she whispered, a request for guidance and strength. When she opened her eyes, it was with a clarity and determination that seemed to charge the very air around her.

The opening chords of "Praise Is What I Do" filled the sanctuary, and Melanie let the spirit move through her as she began to sing. Her voice, rich and soulful, seemed to tap directly into the well of her faith, resonating through the church with a purity that was palpable. As the choir joined in, their harmonies intertwining with hers, the congregation was lifted in a swell of praise that transcended the ordinary Sunday service.

Melanie swayed gently, her whole being immersed in the music. This wasn't just a performance; it was her calling, her way of connecting with something greater than herself. She poured every ounce of her passion into leading the choir, her movements keeping time with the melody, her energy infectious.

As the song built to its powerful climax, Melanie's voice soared, embodying the fire of the Holy Spirit she felt within her. This was more than just leading the church choir; it was a testament to her belief that she was destined for greater things. The final notes rang out, and the church erupted in applause, a chorus of "Amen!" and "Hallelujah!" rising from the pews.

Flushed with the joy of the moment, Melanie stepped down from the altar, her heart full and ready to receive the word of God.

After service Jasmine, her best friend and biggest cheerleader, was already there, her excitement uncontainable. "You were amazing!" Jasmine gushed, her praise underscored by genuine awe. "That high note in the second verse gave me chills. You're meant for bigger stages, Mel."

Laughing, touched by Jasmine's faith in her, Melanie felt a surge of ambition. "Leading worship is where I'm meant to be, but yes, I dream of more. I won't stop until I'm sharing my gift on a much larger scale."

Jasmine's expression turned serious, her support unwavering. "You have a rare talent, Mel, and a heart that seeks to glorify God. Those dreams of yours? They're going to open doors you never imagined."

Grasping Jasmine's hand, Melanie felt a swell of gratitude. For now, her focus was on honing her craft here, in the heart of Havencrest, trusting that the path to greater opportunities would unfold in God's timing.

As they left the sanctuary, Melanie reminisced with Jasmine about her childhood dreams of singing before vast audiences, her voice tinged with a vulnerability she rarely showed. Jasmine's encouragement was a balm to her doubts, a reminder that Melanie's aspirations were not only valid but achievable.

Melanie's dreams, however, were tinged with concerns about balancing her faith and future career, and the fear that her ambitions might stand in the way of finding a partner who shared her values.

Jasmine, ever the voice of reason and faith, reassured her. "God's plan for you includes all the desires of your heart,

Mel. Your future partner will support your dreams, not hinder them."

Their conversation, filled with dreams and doubts, fears and faith, encapsulated the journey Melanie was on—a journey toward realizing her God-given potential, guided by the unwavering support of a friend who believed in her unconditionally.

With Jasmine's words echoing in her heart, Melanie stepped into the fading day, her spirits lifted. The path ahead might be fraught with challenges, but with faith as her compass, she knew she could navigate any storm. Together, they walked on, their friendship a testament to the power of belief and the unshakeable conviction that with God, all things were possible.

One

The Prodigal's Return

Ace Andreas revved his motorcycle, the familiar purr of the engine a stark contrast to the quiet, almost picturesque streets of Havencrest. Rolling back into town felt like flipping through an old photo album—each turn, each landmark, a snapshot of a past life he'd left in the rearview mirror. But here he was, back again, with a mix of apprehension and something that felt suspiciously like anticipation churning in his gut.

The sun was beginning to dip, painting the sky in shades of gold and pink, as he pulled up to Joey's Diner. The place was a Havencrest staple, its neon sign a beacon for the hungry and nostalgic alike. Ace couldn't help but smile as the scent of burgers and fries hit him—the kind of smile that had nothing to do with happiness and everything to do with memories.

"Well, if it isn't the ghost of Havencrest past," Jax bellowed from the heavy duty truck parked next to his bike, his voice rough with years of shouting orders on constructions sites.

Ace's return grin was more reflex than anything. "Guess I couldn't stay away from Joey's world-famous burgers."

“Yeah right, more like you just missed my face,” Tre laughed as he hopped out of the passenger seat of the truck.

Tre's laugh was a sound that seemed to echo back to Ace's teenage years, a simpler time before life got complicated.

The Andreas brothers' reunion was something out of an old movie—complete with bear hugs and backslaps that might've knocked a lesser man to his knees. Jax, the responsible one, had that 'big brother' vibe down to an art, while Tre, the eternal jokester, kept the mood light, deflecting the undercurrent of tension with his quips.

Ace chuckled, following Tre inside with Jax. The scent of sizzling burgers and sweet cherry pies welcomed them. Ace paused, taking it all in. After years on the road, this familiar place felt like coming home.

As they settled into a booth, Ace took a moment to look around. The diner hadn't changed much—same checkered floors, same vinyl seats that had seen better days. It was like stepping back in time, except he wasn't the same kid who used to hang out here, dreaming of nothing bigger than the next Friday night.

Jax and Tre sat across from him, both perusing grease-stained menus like kids in a candy store.

"I gotta say, I love this place," Jax said, eyes scanning the specials.

Ace nodded, memories flooding back. Late nights devouring mountains of fries, laughing until they cried over inside jokes. A lifetime ago.

He glanced around at the other customers, who were eyeing their table curiously. Word must've spread already that the infamous Ace Andreas was back in town.

Their father's reputation still cast a long shadow here. Though he now devoted his life to bringing light to the community, people couldn't forget his dark and violent past. And they wondered if Ace would follow in those footsteps...or forge his own path.

"So Ace, what's next for you once you close this deal?" Tre asked, snapping him from his thoughts. "What really made you come back here, when we all vowed that we never would?"

Ace scrubbed a hand through his short sandy brown hair as he studied his brothers' faces, lined and weary like soldiers back from battle. He knew that just like them, he cut an imposing figure - tall and broad-shouldered, with tattoos snaking up his arms and neck. Not exactly the picture of a deacon's son. But the tattoos covered scars too deep to heal.

Ace had chosen to leave and escape the sins of the past, instead of staying to fight for their father's vision of a new life.

Looking at himself now, he wondered if he'd made the right choice after all.

Jax let out a low whistle. "I don't know, looks like you got more than closing this deal on your mind bro. I'm with Tre... What's her name?"

Ace frowned. "What makes you think there's a her?"

"Come on, I know that look." Tre's eyes glinted with mischief. "Our little Ace is in love."

Ace felt a flush creep up his neck, and he turned away. Love was dangerous. Love had started wars - and ended lives. Losing love could break you and he couldn't let it happen again.

Jax studied him, concern creasing his brow. "You gonna tell us why you're really back here, Ace? You could have sold the casino from anywhere."

Ace met his brother's gaze with a grin. "Dad wanted to see me… and I got some unfinished business."

The diner door swung open, bringing a gust of evening air and a figure from Ace's past—Mary Kincaid, the kind of woman who managed to be both the heart and the unofficial news network of Havencrest. Her eyes landed on Ace, and the look she gave him was one part surprise, two parts disapproval.

"Never thought I'd see the day," she said, sliding into the booth next to him without an invitation. "Ace Andreas, back in the flesh. And here I thought you'd gone and forgotten all about us little people."

Ace could feel the eyes of the diner on them, the weight of expectation heavy in the air. This was it, the moment of truth—was he back as the prodigal son or just another lost soul passing through?

"I'm just here to settle some things," Ace replied, voice steady even as his heart raced. "Havencrest was always gonna be a part of my story, one way or another."

Mary's gaze softened, just a fraction. "Well, you've always been one of ours, no matter where you've been. Just remember, this town's got a long memory, but it's also got a big heart."

As Mary left, Ace found himself staring out the window, the reflections of the diner lights blurring with the fading daylight. Havencrest, with all its small-town charm and hidden depths, was a puzzle he wasn't sure he could solve. But for the first time in a long time, he felt a tug in his chest, a pull towards something that felt like home—or maybe, just maybe, a second chance.

Two

Echoes of the Past

Melanie Barnett's morning kicked off like it always did, in the cozy, sunlit corner of her apartment right in the heart of Havencrest. She had this little ritual, kind of her own sacred moment, where she'd sit down with her well-loved Bible and let the words fill her up. This morning, it was Philippians 4:6 that caught her heart, whispering, "Do not be anxious about anything, but in every situation, by prayer and petition, with thanksgiving, present your requests to God."

As the choir director of the local church and a big supporter of Havencrest's youth through a nonprofit, Melanie pretty much had her plate full. She loved her gig, felt like she was making a difference, but deep down, there was this longing—a kind of ache for a partner who'd share her deep faith and walk the path alongside her.

Her peaceful morning bubble popped with the chirpy ring-tone of her phone. It was Samantha, her go-to for every-thing from fashion fails to faith talks. "Hey girl, how's your morning?" Melanie greeted, her voice warm with affection.

"Hey Mel! Just the usual chaos. I swear, my cat is plotting to take over the world," Sam's laughter bubbled through the phone, light and infectious.

They chatted about their week, shared a laugh over a recent church mishap, and then Sam's tone shifted, becoming more hesitant.

"Mel, there's something you should know... It's about Ace," Sam said cautiously, aware of the old wounds the name might reopen.

Ace. Just the mention of his name had Melanie stumbling through a maze of memories she thought she'd locked up tight. "Yeah?" Melanie managed, her voice a whisper-thin thread.

"I didn't want you to hear it from someone else, but he's back in town." Samantha dropped the bomb, her voice laced with a 'brace yourself' kind of warning.

That news had Melanie's heart doing somersaults. Ace—her once-upon-a-time everything, before he up and vanished, leaving a silence too loud in his wake.

"How'd you find out?" Melanie's curiosity piqued, her heart tangled in a mess of old feelings and unanswered questions.

"Saw him yesterday, roaring back into Havencrest on his bike," Samantha shared, adding a layer of reality to the whole Ace-is-back scenario. "Ran into Tre this morning, and he mentioned Ace is here to stay...or so it seems."

The whole thing had Melanie's emotions running a marathon. Part of her was curious, maybe even a little excited, but then there was this other part, still nursing a bruise or two from Ace's sudden exit years ago.

"Did Tre say why Ace's back?" Melanie probed, her mind racing with possibilities.

"Just mentioned some unfinished business and wanting to reconnect with old friends," Samantha relayed, her voice a mix of caution and curiosity.

Melanie let out a sigh, a cocktail of relief and apprehension swirling inside. Part of her was tempted to see Ace again, to maybe close chapters left open. But then, self-preservation kicked in, whispering warnings to tread carefully.

"Thanks for the heads-up, Sam," Melanie said, a genuine note of gratitude in her voice.

"Anytime, Mel. Just watch your back, okay?" Samantha's concern came through, clear and strong.

With the call wrapped up, Melanie was left with a whirlwind of thoughts. Ace's return wasn't just a blip on her radar—it was a storm brewing on the horizon. And as she headed out to choir practice later that evening, her mind was a battleground of what-ifs and memories.

Choir practice turned out to be the distraction Melanie needed. Music had this way of wrapping her in a warm embrace, letting her pour all those tangled emotions into something beautiful. Leading the choir, her voice blending with others in a harmony that felt like prayer, Melanie found her strength. Each song, each note, was a reminder of her faith's power to heal and hold her together.

After choir practice, Pastor James Harris caught up with Melanie. The pastor had been a pillar of strength and wisdom in her life ever since she joined the church. His kind, gentle demeanor always put her at ease, and tonight was no exception.

"Melanie, you seemed a bit distant today. Everything okay?" he asked, concern etched on his features.

Melanie hesitated for a moment before deciding to share her news. She told him about Ace's return and how it had left her feeling confused and unsure.

"It's just...confusing," she admitted with a sigh. She hadn't really acknowledged her feelings about Ace's return until now, but talking to Pastor Harris made them bubble to the surface.

The pastor placed a comforting hand on her shoulder and gave her an understanding smile. "I can imagine it must be difficult for you," he said gently. "But remember, Melanie, the Lord is close to the brokenhearted."

Melanie nodded, taking comfort in those words. She had always turned to God during tough times, but this felt different somehow. It was like she was being tested; how would she handle seeing Ace again after all these years? Would she let old wounds reopen or would she trust in God and find healing?

"Trust in Him, Melanie," Pastor Harris continued. "He'll guide you through this."

His words brought a sense of peace to Melanie's heart. She knew deep down that whatever happened with Ace, God would be by her side every step of the way.

"Thank you, Pastor Harris," she said sincerely.

He patted her shoulder once more before heading off towards his office. Melanie stayed behind for a few moments longer, soaking in the quiet atmosphere of the church sanctuary.

As she drove home later that night, thoughts of Ace still swirled in her mind, but they were accompanied by a newfound sense of peace and trust in God's plan for her.

Leaving the church, the conversation with Pastor Harris lingered in her mind, mingling with the day's reflections and emotions. Melanie felt a bit steadier, a bit more prepared to face whatever lay ahead. Her faith was her compass, guiding her through life's storms.

That night, seeking further comfort, Melanie turned to Jeremiah 29:11, "For I know the plans I have for you," declares the Lord, "plans to prosper you and not to harm you, plans to give you hope and a future."

Embracing her faith as a shield against the storm of emotions, Melanie found peace in the knowledge that God had great plans for her and she was never alone.

Three

Melodies of Faith and Doubt

So, the thing about small towns like Havencrest is that news travels not just fast but at lightning speed, especially when it involves someone like Ace Andreas making a grand re-entrance. You'd think he was a celebrity, not just a guy who used to be known for his wild days and even wilder motorcycle rides before he disappeared off the face of the earth.

Ace, on his part, was trying to keep a low profile, if you can call riding around on a motorcycle that sounds like a roaring beast "low profile." But deep down, he was wrestling with a cocktail of feelings about being back. It's like he wanted to mend some bridges but wasn't quite sure where to start. Or maybe he was just hoping to run into familiar faces without actually planning it.

One of those faces happened to be Melanie Barnett. Now, Melanie and Ace go way back, back to when they were just kids running around, getting into trouble, and making promises they couldn't keep. Ace had always joked about marrying Melanie one day, an adolescent crush that never quite faded away even when life took them on very different paths.

Fast forward to Sunday morning at the Havencrest Church of Worship. Melanie was there, as usual, her focus on the choir and making sure everything was perfect for the service. Little did she know, she was about to have a blast from the past walk right through those church doors.

Ace, deciding on a whim to attend a service, figured it was as good a place as any to start making amends. Or at least, that's what he told himself. Walking into the church, he felt every bit the prodigal son, half expecting lightning to strike him down the moment he crossed the threshold.

The service was already in full swing when he slipped into the back row, trying to be as inconspicuous as a man with his history could be. But then he saw her—Melanie, leading the choir with such passion and grace, just like he remembered. For a moment, everything else faded away. It was just Melanie's voice filling the space, reminding him of simpler times.

After the service, Melanie was mingling with the congregation, her usual post-service routine, when she spotted him. It was like time stood still. Ace Andreas, looking a little rough around the edges but still the same guy who once promised her the moon.

Their eyes met, and for a second, Melanie thought she might be imagining things. But no, Ace was really here, in the flesh, giving her that half-smile that used to make her heart skip a beat.

"Hey, Mel," Ace said, his voice a mix of nerves and something like hope. It was awkward, the kind of awkward you can't just laugh off.

Melanie, caught somewhere between surprised and wary, managed a, "Ace? What are you doing here?" It came out more accusatory than she intended.

"Just, uh, back in town for a bit. Thought I'd catch a service, you know?" Ace shrugged, trying to play it cool, but Melanie could see right through it.

"What brings you back to town?" she inquired, adding an edge to her words—a protective measure. "What, you've traded motorcycle rides and mafia ties for the goodness of the Lord?"

"Maybe I'm turning over a new leaf, but really just... Business," he said, the word carrying a weight that hinted at stories untold. "And, apparently, running into ghosts from my past."

"More like skeletons," she corrected him quietly, tucking a stray lock of hair behind her ear.

"Is that what we are now?" He stepped closer, bridging the gap with a boldness that bordered on audacity.

"Isn't it?" Melanie challenged taking a step back; her gaze steady but her pulse thrumming a frenetic beat.

For a moment, they stood locked in a silent duet, their body language singing verses of a song unfinished. Then, Melanie broke the connection, turning to leave. "Good luck with your business, Ace," she said, her voice a quiet crescendo of finality.

But as she willed herself to walk away, her hands trembled, and she wondered if some melodies were destined to remain unresolved. Melanie's fists clenched, her nails biting into her palms, a silent reminder of the walls she had meticulously built around herself.

Ace trailed her, making his way around the others leaving service. "I messed up, Mel," he confessed, his voice heavy with regret. "That was a different life, a different me. Can't we at least talk about it?"

The charged silence that fell between them was palpable, even as other church goers walked by, oblivious to the tension that hung in the air. Melanie took a deep breath, her heart pounding like a drumbeat in her chest. She turned and looked into Ace's eyes, searching for a hint of the boy she had once loved, and found a man who had been changed by time and trials.

"Talk?" she echoed softly. "Ace, you left without a word. You turned your back on everything—on us." Her voice trembled with the weight of memories.

"I know," he said softly. "And I live with that regret every single day. But the man standing before you now...he's learned what's important. And it's not too late, is it?" The raw edge to his words tugged at something deep within her.

Melanie took a deep breath, her fingers tracing the worn edges of her Bible. She glanced at the choir loft, each seat a testament to order and predictability, much like her own life had become.

"Forgiveness is one thing," she replied, her voice firm yet gentle. "Forgetting is another."

Her faith had carried her through many storms, including the one Ace had left in his wake. The scripture from Proverbs 17:9 came to mind: "He who covers over an offense promotes love, but whoever repeats the matter separates close friends."

She knew she needed to forgive him for their past to have any chance at reconciliation. Ace ran a hand through his hair, his gaze pleading with her to understand.

"Guess I'm just looking for my own kind of redemption," he admitted, his voice dropping to a near whisper. The raw edge to his words tugged at something deep within her.

She remembered Ace from their youth group days when he would lead worship with fervor and passion that could rival King David himself. Melanie felt her resolve softening as she looked into Ace's eyes—eyes filled with longing and regret—and knew that she couldn't deny him this chance at redemption and reconciliation. As much as it pained her to admit it, there was still a spark between them that refused to be extinguished by time or distance.

"Reconciliation isn't something you're going to find here with me today," she countered gently, attempting to steer the conversation away from dangerous territory while acknowledging his search for something more profound than material possessions could provide.

"Maybe not," he mused thoughtfully, stepping closer to bridge the gap between them. "But maybe it starts with reconnecting with the past."

He reached out as if to brush a piece of lint from her shoulder but stopped short, leaving an electric charge in the air between them. Melanie felt her heart skip a beat at his nearness and took a step back to regain her composure. She couldn't let herself be swept away by emotion; she needed to remain grounded in faith and reason.

They stood there for a moment, the air charged with a decade's worth of unsaid words and unresolved feelings. It was Samantha who eventually broke the tension, pulling Melanie away with a whispered excuse about needing to discuss some church business.

As Melanie walked away, she couldn't help but throw a glance back at Ace, who was watching her leave with an unreadable expression. A part of her—the part that remembered all the good times—wanted to go back and talk to him, to find out why he wanted to reconcile so badly. But another part, the part that had learned to guard her heart, reminded her to be cautious.

Ace's return had thrown her for a loop, dredging up feelings she thought she'd long since buried. As she lay in bed that night, Melanie found herself wondering about the roads not taken, about what could have been if Ace hadn't left all those years ago.

But life had a way of moving on, even if the past refused to stay buried. Melanie knew that whatever reasons Ace truly had for coming back, they were bound to complicate her life in ways she wasn't sure she was ready for. Still, as she drifted off to sleep, a part of her couldn't help but feel a glimmer of hope.

Maybe, just maybe, this was a chance for closure, for answers to the questions that had lingered in the back of her mind for far too long.

Four

The Proposal

Melanie spent the next few days walking an emotional tightrope. The encounter with Ace at church had reopened chapters of her life she thought were firmly closed. She found herself reflecting on their past, the deep connection they once shared, and the pain of his abrupt departure.

Meanwhile, Ace was grappling with his own set of challenges. His return to Havencrest wasn't just a trip down memory lane; it was a journey to confront his past and hopefully forge a new future. The encounter with Melanie had stirred feelings he hadn't anticipated, prompting him to consider what he truly wanted from his return.

At Havencrest Community Center

Melanie was helping organize an upcoming charity event when Samantha walked in, her expression a mix of concern and curiosity.

"Mel, how are you holding up? I saw Ace hanging around Main Street today," Samantha said, getting straight to the point.

Melanie sighed, setting aside a stack of flyers. "It's complicated, Sam. Seeing him again... it's stirred up a lot," she admitted.

"Have you two talked since I helped with your great escape at church?" Samantha asked, leaning against a table.

"He's texts me, my number hasn't changed, but I keep my replies minimal. It's like I'm trying to avoid the big elephant in the room," Melanie replied, her voice tinged with frustration.

At Joey's Diner

Ace found himself at Joey's Diner again, a place that was becoming a refuge of sorts. Jax joined him, sliding into the booth with a look that said he meant business.

"Alright, spill it. You've been back a week, and it's like you're a ghost haunting the place. What's really going on, Ace?" Jax demanded, his tone serious.

Ace took a deep breath. "I've been thinking a lot about why I came back. Seeing Melanie again... it's thrown me for a loop," he confessed.

Jax raised an eyebrow. "Melanie Barnett? I remember you two were inseparable once upon a time."

"Yeah, well, a lot has changed since then," Ace said, stirring his coffee absentmindedly. "I hurt her, Jax. Left without a word. And now, I don't even know where to start making amends."

A Bold Move

Determined to find some closure or perhaps a new beginning, Ace decided to take a bold step. He waited for Melanie after choir practice one evening, his heart racing with a mixture of nerves and determination.

Melanie was surprised to see him, her guard instantly up. "Ace, what are you doing here?" she asked, wary of his intentions.

"I've been doing a lot of thinking," Ace started, his gaze steady on hers. "About us, about the past, and how I left things. I know I can't change what happened, but I want to make things right, Mel."

Melanie's heart skipped a beat, conflicting emotions battling within her. "Ace, I don't know if things can just be 'made right'," she said, her voice soft but firm.

"I know, and I'm not expecting everything to go back to how it was. But, Mel, I was wondering... what if we tried again? Not just picking up where we left off, but starting over?" Ace proposed, the words feeling both right and terrifyingly bold.

Melanie took a step back, the proposal catching her off guard. "Ace, you're talking as if it's that simple. We've both changed. Life has moved on," she pointed out, her mind racing.

"I understand that. I do. But "I'm not the same person I was when I left, Mel. And I see now that my journey led me back here for a reason. It's kind of like what I learned in the men's Bible study the other night, 'Therefore, if anyone is in Christ, he is a new creation. The old has passed away; behold, the new has come'" Ace said, quoting 2 Corinthians 5:17.

Melanie was taken aback by his reference to scripture, a side of Ace she hadn't seen in ages and didn't even think he would still embrace the calling the Lord had on his life. It made her pause, considering his words and the sincerity behind them.

"And what about 'For I know the plans I have for you,' declares the Lord, 'plans to prosper you and not to harm you, plans to give you hope and a future'?" Melanie countered with Jeremiah 29:11. "How do I know this isn't just another detour in your plans, Ace? A detour that's going to leave me hurt and broken again."

"That's just it, Mel. I believe we could be part of each other's plans, the ones He has for us. I'm not asking for an answer right now. Just think about it, please?" Ace pleaded, his earnestness clear.

They stood there, under the soft glow of the streetlamp, the night air carrying the weight of their conversation. Melanie looked at Ace, really looked at him, seeing traces of the boy she once knew in the hardened man before her.

"I'll think about it, Ace. That's all I can promise right now," Melanie said finally, her heart feeling both heavy and light with the possibility of what could be.

As they parted ways that night, both Melanie and Ace were acutely aware of the crossroads they stood at. The proposition of starting anew, of rewriting their story with the wisdom and grace they had found in their separate journeys, was a chance neither had expected.

Melanie lay awake that night, pondering Ace's words, the scriptures they'd volleyed, and the myriad of feelings swirling within her. The thought of opening her heart again, especially to Ace, was daunting. Yet, there was a flicker of hope, a whisper of faith that maybe, just maybe, they could find a way to heal, to grow, and to love anew, in a way that honored both their past and the future they might build together.

In the quiet of the night, Melanie prayed for guidance, for clarity, and for the strength to navigate the path ahead, whatever it might bring. And as she finally drifted off to sleep, the verses they had exchanged lingered in her mind, a reminder that with faith, all things were possible.

FIVE

A Test of Faith

Melanie sat across from Samantha in the cozy corner of the Havencrest Café, the aroma of coffee blending with the warmth of friendship. The café buzzed with the low murmur of conversations and the clink of cups, a backdrop to the serious discussion about to unfold.

"Mel, you've been quiet since you mentioned running into Ace again. Spill it. What's going on in that head of yours?" Samantha probed, her concern evident.

Melanie sighed, tracing the rim of her coffee cup. "I don't know, Sam. Seeing Ace again... it's like reopening a book I thought I closed a long time ago."

Samantha reached across the table, offering a supportive squeeze. "And...?"

"And he's changed, Sam. Or at least, he seems to have. But it's complicated, you know?" Melanie's voice was a mix of confusion and curiosity.

Before Samantha could reply, Melanie's phone buzzed. She glanced at the screen, her expression morphing into surprise. "It's Ace. He wants to meet up. Says he has something important to discuss."

Samantha raised an eyebrow. "And you're going to meet him?"

"I think I should."

The park was Havencrest's little slice of tranquility, with its sprawling lawns and towering oaks. It was here, on a bench overlooking the duck pond, that Melanie found Ace waiting. The setting sun cast long shadows, painting the scene in a soft, golden light.

"Ace," Melanie greeted, her voice steady despite the gale of emotions swirling within her.

"Melanie. Thanks for coming," Ace replied, standing to greet her. His voice held a hint of nervousness she hadn't expected.

They sat, the space between them charged with a tension that spoke volumes of their past.

"I'll get straight to the point," Ace began, his gaze fixed on the pond. "I've been doing a lot of thinking since I came back... about us, about our conversations, about everything that happened."

Melanie nodded, signaling him to continue, her heart beating a rapid tattoo against her ribs.

"I was a fool, Mel. Leaving the way I did, without a word... I regret that more than you can imagine," Ace confessed, his voice low.

Melanie felt a tight knot in her chest loosen slightly at his words. "Regret doesn't change the past, Ace."

"I know, I know it doesn't. But it's brought me to a realization. I want to make things right, not just with you, but with my life. I've been reading outside of church, you know, the Bible. Came across Luke 15:7, 'I say to you that likewise there will be more joy in heaven over one sinner who repents than over ninety-nine just persons who need no repentance.' It hit me hard, Mel."

Melanie was taken aback by his admission, the scripture reference catching her off guard. "Ace, I... That's unexpected."

"There's more," Ace continued, hesitating for a moment. "I've been given a chance to start over, to do something meaningful. But I need a partner, someone who shares my vision, my... faith journey."

Melanie's heart skipped a beat. "What are you saying, Ace?"

"I'm saying... Would you really consider starting over with me? Not just picking up where we left off, but something new. A partnership, in every sense."

Melanie's mind raced. This was the last thing she expected. "You're talking about marriage?"

"In a way, yes. But not just marriage. A true partnership, where we both contribute, grow, and maybe... heal," Ace clarified, his eyes meeting hers, pleading for understanding.

The proposal left Melanie reeling. The man before her bore little resemblance to the Ace she remembered. His words, his demeanor, even the way he spoke of faith and future, spoke of a transformation that was hard to ignore.

"Proverbs 3:5-6, 'Trust in the Lord with all your heart, and lean not on your own understanding; in all your ways submit to Him, and He will make your paths straight.' That's what I'm trying to do, Mel. I'm asking you to trust in the possibility of a new path for us," Ace said, his voice imbued with sincerity.

Melanie took a deep breath, the scripture echoing in her mind. The idea of embarking on a new journey with Ace, one grounded in faith and mutual growth, was both terrifying and exhilarating.

"Ace, I... I need time to think about this. It's a lot to take in," Melanie finally said, her voice barely above a whisper.

"I understand. Take all the time you need, Mel. I just want you to know, I'm serious about this. About us. And about making a difference, together," Ace replied, standing up. "I'll be at church on Sunday. Maybe we can talk more after the service?"

Melanie nodded, a tumult of emotions rendering her speechless. As Ace walked away, she remained seated, the fading light of day reflecting the turmoil and tentative hope within her.

The proposal was unexpected, a curveball that Melanie couldn't have anticipated. Yet, as she walked back through the quiet streets of Havencrest, she couldn't shake the feeling that perhaps, in the midst of all the uncertainty, there lay a seed of possibility. A chance for redemption, for love, and for a future that neither of them could have imagined alone.

But the decision wasn't hers to make in isolation. Prayer, reflection, and, most importantly, a conversation with God were needed before she could even begin to consider Ace's proposal. The path ahead was unclear, but Melanie knew that with faith as her guide, the right way forward would reveal itself in time.

As the night settled over Havencrest, Melanie found solace in her prayers, seeking guidance and strength from the One who had always been her constant. The scripture from Proverbs 3:5-6 resonated deeply, a reminder to trust in the Lord's plan, even when the road ahead seemed shrouded in mystery.

Tomorrow was another day, and with it would come clarity and perhaps the courage to embrace whatever lay ahead. For now, Melanie held onto her faith, the words of scripture a beacon in the night, guiding her toward a future filled with hope and the promise of new beginnings.

Six

Harmony Amidst Discord

The days following Ace's bold proposition found Melanie in a state of reflection, her thoughts a tangled mess of past memories and future possibilities. The idea of starting anew with Ace, of all people, was both unsettling and oddly comforting. She found herself noticing the little changes in him, like the way his tattoos peeked out from under his sleeves—each inked line a story, a remnant of his journey since they'd last been close.

Meanwhile, Ace was doing some soul-searching of his own. His tattoos, once markers of a rebellious phase, now felt like a map of his life's detours and destinations. He wondered if Melanie could ever truly accept him and his past, ink and all.

At the Havencrest Café

Melanie and Samantha met up for their usual coffee catch-up, but today's conversation veered into deeper waters.

"So, I met with Ace at the park the other night. He basically asked me marry him," Melanie started, her voice hesitant.

Samantha nearly choked on her coffee. "He what? Mel, that's huge! What did he say?"

"He talked about starting over, about being different now," Melanie said, tracing the rim of her coffee cup. "He even quoted scripture, Sam. It was... surprising."

Samantha leaned in; her curiosity piqued. "Do you believe him? People can change, Mel."

"I want to, I really do. It's just hard to reconcile the Ace I knew with the man he claims to be now. And his tattoos... they're like a visual reminder of all the reasons we drifted apart."

"But maybe they're also a reminder of what he's overcome," Samantha suggested gently. "Everyone has a past, Mel. It's what we do with our future that counts."

Melanie sighed, the weight of her friend's words sinking in. Could she really open her heart to Ace again, knowing all the ways it could go wrong?

****Across Town****

Ace met up with Jax at their old hangout spot, a quiet park overlooking the river. The setting sun cast a golden glow, illuminating the ink on Ace's arms, each tattoo a chapter in his story.

"Melanie's been on my mind, Jax. I can't shake the feeling that this is my second chance," Ace confessed, rolling up his sleeves and looking down at the tapestry of ink covering his skin.

Jax followed his gaze, nodding. "Those tattoos... they're a part of you, Ace. Just like your history with Melanie. If you're serious about this, you've got to be honest with her—and yourself."

Ace knew Jax was right. If he and Melanie were going to have any chance at a future, he'd need to lay all his cards on the table, tattoos and all.

A Chance Meeting

The community center was buzzing with the usual afternoon chaos when Ace walked in, his presence causing a brief lull in the noise as people turned to look at the newcomer. Melanie, in the midst of organizing a mountain of donations, felt a jolt of surprise at the sight of him. "Ace, what are you doing here?" she asked, trying to mask her confusion with a casual tone.

Ace, dressed down in jeans and a tee that did little to hide his muscular build or the tapestry of tattoos along his arms, gave her a sheepish grin. "I figured I could lend a hand. You know, try to do some good in the neighborhood," he said, his eyes searching hers for a sign of acceptance.

Melanie hesitated for a moment, studying him. The tattoos, once a point of contention, now seemed like a visual journal of his life's journey. "Alright, you can start by helping me sort these boxes," she directed, handing him a stack of labels and a marker.

As they worked side by side, Ace couldn't help but be drawn into the rhythm of the community center's daily life. Kids ran back and forth, some stopping to see what they were doing, their curiosity piqued by the new face.

"Whoa, mister, your tattoos are cool!" one little boy exclaimed, his eyes wide as he traced the outlines of a dragon winding its way up Ace's forearm.

Ace chuckled, bending down to the boy's level. "Thanks, buddy. Each one tells a story. Like this dragon here—it's about strength and overcoming tough times," he explained, enjoying the kid's fascination.

Melanie watched the interaction, a warmth growing in her chest. It was a side of Ace she hadn't seen before, one that effortlessly connected with the innocence and curiosity of the children. "You're good with them," she commented, not without a hint of surprise.

Ace stood up, meeting her gaze. "I guess I've got a soft spot for kids. They see the world in such a straightforward way, you know?"

They moved through the afternoon, Ace sharing stories behind his tattoos when asked, each tale a piece of the puzzle that was his life. Melanie found herself drawn into his world, the barriers between them slowly dissolving with every shared laugh and story.

At one point, as they were moving a particularly heavy box, Ace's sleeve rode up, revealing an intricate piece that Melanie hadn't seen before—a compass encircled by a quote. "What's this one?" she asked, nodding toward the design.

Ace followed her gaze, his expression softening. "It's a reminder that no matter how lost I get, there's always a way back. It's Luke 1:79 **"Shining on those in the darkness, those sitting in the shadow of death, Then showing us the way, one foot at a time, down the path of peace." The MSG**

Melanie paused, struck by the depth of the sentiment. "Th at's... really profound, Ace."

He shrugged, a bashful smile playing on his lips. "Had a lot of time to think about the paths I've taken. This tattoo's a promise to myself—to find the right way, even when it feels like I'm wandering in the dark."

As the day wound down and the last box was sorted, Melanie turned to Ace, a newfound respect in her eyes. "Today was a good day, Ace. Thank you for helping out here, for sharing a bit of your story with me...and the kids. It was... eye-opening.""

Ace wiped his hands on his jeans, looking around the now-organized space with a sense of accomplishment. " Anytime, Mel. I just want the chance to prove I'm not the same guy who left all those years ago. I meant what I said, Mel. About wanting to make things right. Today was a step in that direction, wasn't it?"

Melanie nodded, her heart lighter than it had been in days. "It was, Ace. It definitely was."

They locked up the community center together, the setting sun casting a soft glow over the day's end. The time they'd spent together had opened Melanie's eyes to the changes in Ace, to the man he was becoming. And as they went their separate ways, both felt a flicker of hope that perhaps this was the beginning of a new chapter, one where past mistakes could be forgiven and a new future could be forged, together.

Driving home, Melanie reflected on the day, on Ace's tattoos and the stories they held—a vivid reminder that change was possible, that people could grow and evolve. And maybe, just maybe, so could whatever was blossoming between them.

Seven

A Crescendo of Courage

After the day at the community center, Melanie found herself nursing emotions she hadn't expected to feel again, especially not for Ace. It was as if the man with the dragon tattoo, and stories etched in ink across his skin, was a stranger she was getting to know all over again.

A few days later, Melanie and Samantha decided to grab a late breakfast at the local diner, a spot that had become their unofficial meeting place for life's ups and downs.

"So, spill," Samantha prompted, sipping her coffee with an expectant look. "How are things... evolving with Ace?"

Melanie played with her spoon, the clinking sound a stalling tactic as she gathered her thoughts. "It's complicated, Sam. He's not the same guy who left, and the more I see him, the more I realize that. He's... different."

"Different good or different bad?" Samantha probed, her eyebrows raised in that way that meant she wanted details.

"Different good, I think," Melanie admitted, a small smile tugging at her lips. "He's been helping out at the community center, connecting with the kids, and sharing parts of his story. It's like he's genuinely trying to make amends, not just with me but with himself."

Samantha nodded, her expression softening. "That's a big deal, Mel. People change, and it sounds like Ace really is trying. What are you going to do about it?"

Melanie sighed, the weight of the decision heavy on her heart. "I'm not sure yet. Part of me wants to see where this could go, to give him a chance. But there's another part that's scared of getting hurt again."

"Trust your gut, Mel. But remember, forgiveness is powerful. Maybe it's time for a new chapter for both of you," Samantha encouraged, reaching across the table to squeeze Melanie's hand.

Later that week, Ace invited Melanie to join him for a walk in the park, a neutral ground where the echoes of their past might not loom so large. Melanie agreed, curiosity and a budding hope guiding her decision.

The park was quiet, with only the sound of leaves rustling in the gentle breeze accompanying their steps. Ace seemed nervous, a stark contrast to his usual confident demeanor.

"I wanted to thank you for the other day, at the community center," Ace began, his voice tinged with sincerity. "It meant a lot, being able to help and... to spend time with you."

Melanie looked at him, noticing the way the sunlight caught the edges of his tattoos, highlighting the intricate designs. "It was eye-opening, Ace. Seeing you in a different light, it's made me rethink a lot of things."

Ace stopped walking, turning to face her. "Mel, I know I can't erase the past, but I'm hoping we can build something new. Not forgetting what happened, but maybe... moving forward, together?"

The vulnerability in his eyes was something Melanie hadn't seen before. It made her heart ache for the pain they'd both endured, for the years lost to silence and misunderstanding.

"Moving forward means trust, Ace. It means opening up and being honest about the hard stuff," Melanie said, her own vulnerability mirroring his.

"I know, and I'm ready for that. For what it's worth, I've been thinking about getting a new tattoo," Ace shared, a half-smile appearing. "One that symbolizes this new chapter, the journey of making things right. With you, with my family, with myself."

The idea of Ace marking this moment of change so permanently gave Melanie pause, a visual testament to his commitment to change and growth. "I'd like to see that, when you're ready to share it," she said, a tentative peace settling between them.

As they resumed their walk, the conversation flowed more freely, touching on memories of their shared past but also on their individual journeys since then. Ace talked about his mafia past, giving Melanie the PG version of some of the things he had witnessed; his travels and the places that had left marks on his soul as indelible as the ink on his skin. Melanie shared her own growth, the challenges, and triumphs of leading the choir and her work with the youth.

It was during these moments, with the setting sun casting a warm glow around them, that Melanie realized the depth of the change in both of them. They were no longer the teenagers who had dreamt of a future together, nor were they strangers. They were two people, shaped by life's trials and tribulations, finding their way back to each other.

Before they parted ways, Ace turned to Melanie, a seriousness in his gaze. "I'm here for the long haul, Mel. I want to be someone you can rely on, someone who adds to your life, not just a reminder of the past."

Melanie nodded, the promise in his words igniting a flicker of hope within her. "Let's take it one day at a time, Ace. See where this path leads us."

As Melanie walked home, her mind replayed their conversation, the openness and honesty a balm to the old wounds she'd carried for so long. She didn't know what the future held, but for the first time in years, she felt open to exploring it, with Ace by her side.

That night, as she sat by her window, Melanie found herself praying not just for guidance but for the courage to embrace this new chapter, whatever it might bring. The words of Philippians 4:13 strengthened her resolve: "I can do all things through Christ who strengthens me."

And as she closed her eyes, Melanie felt a sense of peace envelop her, the kind that comes from knowing you're exactly where you're meant to be, at the crossroads of past and future, ready to step forward in faith.

EIGHT

The Power of Grace

Over the next few weeks, Havencrest felt smaller to Ace, each street corner, each familiar face reminding him of paths once taken and those yet to explore. His return had stirred something within him, a mix of nostalgia and a newfound yearning for change that he couldn't quite shake off.

The following Sunday, Ace found himself sitting in a pew at the back of the church, the sermon washing over him in waves of comfort and challenge. He wasn't sure what he was looking for, but something about the familiar songs and Pastor Harris's words felt like a balm to his restless spirit.

After the service, as people milled around, sharing greetings and plans for the week, Melanie approached him, a tentative smile on her lips.

"I'm happy to see you here again," she said, her tone light but curious.

Ace met her gaze, finding a sense of calm in her presence. "Yeah, well, It's all a part of my journey. It's led me here, I guess."

Melanie nodded, understanding the significance of his words. "Change isn't easy, but it's often where we find our true selves. I'm glad you're giving yourself that chance."

Their conversation flowed more easily than before, touching on topics from the mundane to the deeply personal. Ace found himself sharing more with Melanie than he had with anyone in a long time, the words coming more freely in the safety of her understanding.

As they parted ways, Ace felt a stirring within him, a sense of purpose beginning to take root. He wasn't yet sure where this path would lead, but for the first time in a long time, he was ready to find out.

In the days that followed, Ace threw himself into community work, volunteering at the center, working on closing the casino deal that brought him back home, and even joining a church group focused on outreach. The more he gave of himself, the more he felt a sense of belonging, of coming home in a way he hadn't anticipated.

One evening, sitting on the porch of his family's home, Ace found himself deep in thought when Jax joined him, a knowing look in his eye.

"You've been quiet," Jax finally broke the silence, casting a line into the water. "More than usual. What's on your mind?"

Ace watched the water ripple, gathering his thoughts. "I've been thinking about... everything. Coming back, seeing Melanie, the way people look at me like I'm still that youngin' who left all those years ago."

Jax nodded, understanding the weight of those words. "Havencrest has a long memory, but people change, Ace. You've changed."

"It's not just about changing, Jax. It's about making things right," Ace said, his voice carrying a hint of determination that had been absent before. "Being back at the church, helping out with Melanie at the community center... It's opened my eyes to a lot I've been ignoring."

Jax turned to him, a serious look on his face. "So, what are you going to do about it?"

"I don't know yet. But I feel like there's a path for me here, something I'm meant to do, to be," Ace admitted, feeling the weight of his words. "I just never expected that path might lead me back to church, of all places."

"You're different, Ace. In a good way," Jax observed, taking a seat beside him. "I can see it, the change. It suits you."

Ace smiled, looking out at the setting sun painting the sky in shades of orange and pink. "It feels good getting into the Word – developing my relationship with Christ, Jax. Like I'm finally starting to understand who I'm meant to be."

"The church, huh?" Jax chuckled softly. "Never thought I'd hear you say that. But if it feels right, if it brings you some peace, then don't let anyone pull you from your path."

Ace let out a sigh, the tension in his shoulders easing slightly. "Yeah."

"And Melanie?" Jax asked, the question hanging between them like an unspoken understanding.

Ace's smile widened, warmth spreading through his chest at the thought of her. "Melanie... she's a big part of this, I think. She sees me, the real me, not just the mistakes I've made."

Jax clapped him on the back, a gesture of brotherly support. "Then don't let her go, Ace. Not everyone gets a second chance."

As the night fell over Havencrest, Ace felt a peace settle over him, a clarity about his place in the world that had eluded him for so long. He knew the road ahead wouldn't be easy, but with faith, hard work, and maybe a little bit of grace, he was ready to walk it, one step at a time.

Nine

Bonds Rekindled

After a soul stirring Sunday service, the late afternoon sun was just hitting that perfect spot in the sky, you know, where everything looks a bit like it's glowing?

That's how it was when Ace's Audi, all sleek and shiny, pulled back up in front of Melanie's place. He's been doing this every Sunday for the last few months, picking her up for service and dropping her back off, but today felt different somehow.

He parked and did that thing where he walks around to open her door—a gentleman move he's been keeping up consistently. Melanie stepped out, her hand lingering on the door for a second longer than necessary, her eyes meeting his.

"Thanks for the ride," she said, her voice steady but her heart doing somersaults.

Ace locked eyes with her, those honey-colored eyes of his lighting up with something that looked a lot like excitement.

"I'll be back at five," he said, that familiar, cocky grin of his making an appearance. "Dress fancy, Mel. I'm taking you somewhere special tonight, and it's not just any place in town."

Watching his car drive away, Melanie couldn't help the smile that danced on her lips. Ace always had a knack for surprises, but this felt different, more thoughtful. It was a side of him she was only just beginning to get used to, and she had to admit, she kind of loved it.

Right on the dot at five, Ace was back, just as he promised. Melanie caught sight of him from behind the curtains, stepping out of the car with a grace she couldn't recall from their younger days. In his hand was a bouquet of lilies, her favorites, a silent testament to his attentiveness.

"Right on time," commented Sam, Melanie's ever-watchful best friend, without taking her eyes off her book.

"Wouldn't expect anything less," Melanie replied, smoothing out her dress before heading to the door.

Opening it, she found Ace on the other side, and for a moment, he seemed lost for words. There she stood, radiant, her dress accentuating her curves, her curls falling softly over her shoulders. The evening sun cast a halo around her, and Ace was struck by her beauty—a sight so stunning it left him momentarily speechless.

"Wow, Melanie... you look," he paused, his gaze intense, the tattoos on his neck shifting as he searched for the right words, "absolutely stunning."

A blush crept up Melanie's cheeks at the compliment. "Thank you," she managed, taking the lilies. There was a spark in her eyes, a light that seemed to make them shine even brighter. "These are beautiful. Let me just put them in water."

"Like you," Ace murmured, almost too quietly for her to catch.

From the living room, Sam's voice cut through the moment. "Hi, Ace," she said, eyeing him with a mix of curiosity and protective skepticism.

"Sam," Ace nodded, a brief flash of nerves visible despite his usual confidence.

Melanie returned, her steps light, and together they stepped out into the evening, ready for whatever the night might hold.

The drive to the restaurant was filled with a comfortable hum of anticipation. They talked and laughed, sharing stories from the past and hopes for the future. Ace was different, Melanie thought. There was a depth to him now, a sincerity that she couldn't help but be drawn to.

"Remember those choir competitions we used to stress over?" Melanie asked, a laugh escaping her as she thought back to their high school days.

Ace let out a hearty laugh, the sound warm and genuine. "How could I forget? You were always so determined to win."

Their conversation was a melody of its own, notes of nostalgia and new beginnings weaving together in a song that felt both familiar and entirely new.

As they arrived at the restaurant, Melanie couldn't shake the feeling that this was more than just a dinner date. It was a step towards something greater, a leap of faith into a future where the past didn't dictate their course.

And as they sat across from each other, sharing stories and dreams under the soft glow of the restaurant lights, Melanie realized that this evening was a gift—a chance to see Ace not just for who he had been, but for the man he was becoming.

TEN

Refrains of Resilience

The soft glow of the chandelier above cast a warm golden hue on the white tablecloth, and for a moment, Melanie was taken by the elegance of the intimate steakhouse. Ace sat across from her, his broad shoulders outlined by the tailored fit of his dark suit, a stark contrast to the Ace she remembered in leather jackets and defiant smirks. Now, he held a composure that felt both foreign and familiar.

"So, I've been going to the Men's Bible Study group," Ace began, his eyes holding a spark of mirth. "You wouldn't believe it, but last week Pastor Mike somehow managed to tie the story of David and Goliath to his misadventures in fishing."

"How on earth did he manage that?" Melanie chuckled, her big brown eyes lighting up with curiosity.

"Let's just say, he compared facing the giant fish on his line to facing our own giants in life. It was hilarious but... pretty insightful, too." Ace's grin widened, and it was clear the memory brought him joy.

Melanie watched him speak, noticing how his tattoos peeked out from under his crisp shirt sleeves, an intriguing contrast to the vulnerability he now showed. His laughter was rich and genuine – so different from the cocky, domineering presence she remembered.

"Faith has a way of turning even the simplest things into profound lessons," Melanie said thoughtfully, swirling the wine in her glass before taking a sip. Her heart felt strangely light, as if lifted by the harmonies of a choir.

"Exactly," Ace agreed. He leaned forward, resting his elbows on the table, his gaze intent upon her. "What about you, Mel? What role does faith play in your life these days?"

"Faith is a journey, Ace. We all walk it at our own pace," Melanie offered gently, her voice soothing as a lullaby.

"Thanks to you, my family, our church, I feel like I'm finally walking in the right direction," Ace admitted, his voice low and filled with something that sounded like hope. "Believe it or not, I've been doing a lot more listening these days." Ace leaned forward, his elbows resting on the table, and Melanie could see the sincerity etched into the lines of his face. "It's helping me understand things...about faith, life, even us."

"Us?" The word slipped out of Melanie before she could stop it, and she felt her cheeks flush with heat as though they'd been brushed by the steam rising from their entrees.

"Maybe that's a conversation for another time," he said quickly, deflecting with a grace she hadn't known he possessed.

Their dishes arrived, placed before them with a flourish of silverware and polite smiles from the waiter. For a moment, the conversation halted as they offered thanks for the meal, their heads bowed in silent prayer. When they looked up again, there was a new understanding in the air—one that spoke of shared beliefs, mutual respect, and the delicate beginnings of trust rekindled.

The air around them felt charged with possibility, with the promise of new beginnings and the courage to face the uncertainties ahead. They shared a look, a silent vow to tread this new path together, hand in hand, with faith as their guide.

As the evening ended, and they stepped out of the restaurant into the cool night air, Melanie and Ace knew that the road ahead would be fraught with challenges. But for the first time, they faced those challenges not as two separate individuals, but as a united front, fortified by love, faith, and the unwavering belief in second chances.

Walking Melanie to her door, the night seemed to hold its breath, the stars twinkling above like a celestial audience to their unfolding story. Ace paused, turning to face her, the soft porch light illuminating his features.

"Mel, I know we've got a lot to work through, but I want you to know, I'm here for the long haul. I'm committed to this, to us," he said, his voice imbued with a resolve that resonated deep within Melanie's heart.

Melanie looked up at him, the flicker of hope in her eyes glowing brighter. "And I'm with you, Ace. We'll take it one step at a time, together."

They stood there, in the quiet of the night, wrapped in a sense of peace and the promise of what was to come. It was a beginning, delicate and new, like the first tentative notes of a song yet to be sung—a melody of redemption, love, and the infinite grace of new beginnings.

As Ace drove away, Melanie watched until his car disappeared into the night. She whispered a prayer of thanks, not just for the evening they'd shared, but for the journey they were about to embark on—a journey of faith, forgiveness, and the beautiful complexity of love reborn.

Inside, the house was quiet, Sam had long since retired for the night, leaving Melanie alone with her thoughts. She sniffed the lilies Ace had given her, their fragrance sweet and comforting, a tangible reminder of the evening's promises.

Climbing the stairs to her room, Melanie felt a lightness she hadn't experienced in years. The future was uncertain, yes, but it was theirs to shape, a canvas on which they would paint their story with strokes of patience, understanding, and unwavering faith.

As she drifted off to sleep, Melanie's heart was full, buoyed by the belief that, together, they could face whatever lay ahead. With God as their guide, and love as their compass, there was no storm they couldn't weather, no obstacle too great to overcome.

And in that quiet, sacred space between wakefulness and dreams, Melanie felt a profound sense of gratitude. For second chances, for the power of forgiveness, and for the unexpected paths that lead us back to the ones we love.

Eleven

The Blueprint of Change

As Ace stepped into the church, the door's creak echoed in the quiet space, mirroring the rhythm of his heart. The familiar smells of polished wood and leather-bound hymnals enveloped him, a stark contrast to the life he once knew. This was his fourth visit to the men's study group, each session peeling back the layers of his past, feeling like a fresh start.

Under his breath, Ace whispered a prayer, "Lord, help me find my path."

"Welcome back, Ace!" Samuel's voice boomed from across the room, breaking through Ace's introspection with the warmth of welcome.

"Thanks, Samuel," Ace responded, his voice carrying a mix of gratitude and determination as he made his way to join the group. Despite his imposing presence, there was a humbleness to him that hadn't been there before.

He scanned the group, each man deeply engaged in discussion, their hands animated as they explored the night's topic. Touching the tattoos that marked his journey, Ace felt a blend of unease and anticipation.

"Can I join in?" he asked, his voice softer than usual, hinting at the vulnerability beneath his tough exterior.

"Of course," came the reply, as the men made space for him. Settling into his chair, Ace felt out of place yet drawn to the promise of redemption and change they discussed.

Pastor James introduced the evening's theme of transformation, drawing parallels between Saul's conversion to Paul and the potential for change in their own lives.

Ace listened, his own story reflecting back at him through their words. "To see clearly, we must first be broken," someone mentioned, resonating with Ace. He was familiar with being broken but seeing clearly? That was uncharted territory.

"God calls the willing, not just the able," Pastor James said directly to Ace, a statement that sparked something within him. Was it possible for someone with his past to be made anew?

The group discussed the tools of change: faith, community, and prayer. "Renovation," Ace repeated, the concept hitting close to home. Maybe what he was seeking was not just change but a complete rebuild of his life.

The group's discussion, filled with personal insights and struggles, made Ace rub his tattooed arm, a physical reminder of his journey. "Being broken to see clearly," someone mentioned, and it struck a chord with Ace. He was all too familiar with being broken but seeing clearly? That was new.

Pastor James caught his eye, "God equips those He calls, Ace. It's not about being ready; it's about being willing."

"Tools," Ace pondered, the concept of being equipped by something greater than himself was both foreign and fascinating. Faith, community, prayer - the essentials for rebuilding.

The idea of renovation struck deep. "Tearing down the old to build anew," Ace mused, surprised at his own analogy.

As the meeting continued, the sense of belonging grew. This was the beginning of something new, a path he was just starting to navigate.

The conversations flowed into deeper waters of forgiveness. "It's about letting go," Pastor James said, a concept that Ace found both challenging and liberating. The discussion shifted to the power of forgiving oneself, a concept as daunting as it was necessary for true freedom.

"Seventy-seven times," the group echoed, a reminder of the boundless nature of forgiveness. Ace tasted the words, their significance sinking in. The act of letting go, of freeing oneself from the chains of past grievances, was a theme that resonated deeply.

"Where the Spirit of the Lord is, there is freedom," Pastor James reminded them, a statement that prompted Ace to consider the real meaning of freedom. Could he truly find liberation in forgiveness?

As the group dispersed, Ace lingered, the weight of his past and the possibility of a new future pressing down on him. Seeking guidance, he asked Pastor James for a moment of prayer.

Together, they prayed, Pastor James's words a solid anchor in the tumult of Ace's thoughts. "Lead me on the right path," Ace found himself asking, a genuine desire for change and clarity in his heart.

This was a new beginning, marked not by the assurance of immediate transformation but by the willingness to embark on the journey.

Ace stepped out into the waning evening, feeling kinda like a man on a mission. He pulled out his phone, which suddenly felt like a strange new gadget in his hands.

First up was a call to his lawyer. "Hey Mark, it's Ace. Let's push forward with selling the casino. Gotta move fast on this."

His voice was firm, his intent clear. Next call? A real estate agent known for dealing with commercial properties. "Hey, it's Ace Andreas here. I'm looking to dive into a new venture, something that's all about giving back to the community," he explained, his plans for a brighter future driving the conversation.

After wrapping up his calls and penciling in some meetings, Ace took a moment to lean on his car, his mind drifting to Melanie. Their past was a mixtape of highs and lows, but that bridge would be crossed when he got to it.

For now, he focused on the progress in his hands, the documents in his briefcase marking the end of his casino days and the start of something way bigger. "It's not just about leaving the past behind," he mused to himself. "It's about stepping into the future I'm meant for."

With a contented smile, Ace jumped into his car, ready for the road ahead, knowing every ending was just a brief pause before the next big thing.

The next day at the bank, Ace laid his plans on the table, locking eyes with the bank manager. "Look, my past is exactly why this will work. I know the game of risk better than anyone," he confidently stated, his past playing the unlikely hero in his pitch for a community center.

The manager was all ears, especially when Ace rolled out his blueprints for a youth sports and music complex. "This isn't about making a quick buck. It's about investing in what really matters—people."

As the meeting winded down and Ace found himself alone, he couldn't shake off the nagging doubts. "You're with me on this, right, God?" he whispered, seeking some divine reassurance that he was on the right path.

Then, his phone buzzed. A message from one of the guys from the study group popped up: "Hang in there. You've got this, and we've got you."

That brought a grin to Ace's face. It was nice, knowing he wasn't going solo on this journey. "Alright, time to get to work," he said to himself, rolling up his sleeves to dive back into his plans.

In the days that followed, Ace was on fire, nailing down leases, shaking hands with local business owners, and getting the right people for the job. Every decision felt like a beat in the new soundtrack of his life.

When a potential buyer for the casino quizzed him about letting go, Ace didn't miss a beat. "It's time for a new legacy," he declared, the past loosening its grip with every word.

Even as old temptations whispered his name, Ace held fast to his faith, the new melody of his life unfolding—a blend of hope, hard work, and heart.

Standing in his new space, the future site of something amazing, Ace couldn't help but let out a small prayer. "Let this place be a beacon of Your love," he said, already envisioning the community coming together here, in this very room.

His phone rang, and it was Lucas from the local youth program, already hearing about Ace's plans and hoping to get in on the action.

"Count on it, Lucas. This place is here for the entire community, especially the church," Ace assured him, his heart full, knowing he was making a real difference.

As he ended the call, Ace looked around the empty room, imagining the smiles, the laughter, and the lives he was about to change.

“Guide me through this, God," he prayed quietly, ready to tackle whatever came next with a heart full of hope and hands ready to build a better tomorrow.

"Here’s to second chances," he whispered to the empty room, to himself, to God. A smile creeping up as he thought about the endless possibilities. Ace Andreas, once a man regulated to the shadows and doing the work of the enemy, was now stepping fully into the light, cueing up the first note of a brand-new life symphony all for the glory of the Lord.

TWELVE

Building the Future

As the evening light poured into the room, Ace was on a mission. Towering and built like a fortress, his inked skin peeked out from under his sleeves as he reached for a basket on the counter. The room was filled with the soft scents of lavender and beeswax from the candles he'd picked out.

"Okay, let's see," he talked to himself, ticking off items in his head. "Blanket, candles..." He carefully placed each item in the basket, his usual rough edges softened by the care he put into each movement.

He packed Melanie's favorites with a smile: cornbread muffins, honey butter, and brie. He remembered how she loved mixing the honey's sweetness with the brie's creaminess, a flavor combo she introduced him to.

Folding a blanket neatly—a trick from his days of needing to pack and move quickly—he imagined it wrapped around Melanie, bringing her close in a moment of comfort.

Checking his phone, he quickly typed out a message to Melanie:

Head over to my parent's. Got something to show you.

Hesitation hit him as he was about to send the message. Could he, with his past, really hope for a second shot with someone as good-hearted as Melanie? Pushing doubt aside, he sent the message and focused back on his preparations.

Meanwhile, Melanie's phone buzzed on her table, pulling her away from her work. Seeing Ace's name sent her heart racing. She read his message, feeling a mix of excitement and nervousness.

"God," she whispered, hoping for guidance, "lead me right." Faith had always been her guiding star, and now it seemed to point her towards Ace, towards uncertainty.

Standing up, she steadied herself in the mirror, trying to find confidence in her reflection. "Time to see what this is about," she told her reflection, a mix of resolve and hope in her voice as she typed her reply.

On my way!

Locking her door behind her, Melanie felt a familiar sense of hope. The same hope that had buoyed her when she first sent her song lyrics off. Maybe, just maybe, this was the beginning of a new chapter with Ace.

As she drove off into the sunset, she prayed for wisdom and protection, her heart open to the possibilities of what might come from this candlelit surprise.

Pulling up to the Andreas estate, Melanie was struck again by its imposing beauty. It was like stepping into a different world, one filled with memories both sweet and sour.

"Alright, here we go," she steadied herself, stepping out into the evening. Ace's voice greeted her before she could even close her car door, a mix of excitement and something new, a softness, in his tone.

"Hey, Ace," she replied back, nerves dancing in her stomach.

"Thanks for coming," he said, his presence as commanding as ever, yet there was a warmth there that hadn't been before.

The hug he gave her was firm but gentle, a silent acknowledgment of everything that had passed between them and the fragile hope for what might still be.

He led her through the yard to a setup under the old oak tree, the setting sun making his eyes glow. It felt like stepping into a different world, one where the past didn't have quite the same hold on them.

Climbing up to the treehouse, Ace's hand was there to help her, a simple touch that sparked a flurry of emotions. Inside, the candlelit space was cozy and inviting, a testament to Ace's efforts to make the night special.

"This is amazing, Ace," she couldn't help but admire the scene before her, the warmth of the candles casting a soft glow over everything.

Ace's preparation, down to her favorite snacks, spoke volumes. It was an evening crafted with care, each detail a note in the melody he was hoping to compose with her, a song of reconciliation second chances.

As they settled into the evening, the treehouse around them felt like a cocoon, shielding them from the world outside. It was a chance for new beginnings, a moment suspended in time where the past could be acknowledged but not allowed to dictate their future.

Their conversation meandered through memories and hopes, the soft glow of the candles casting everything in a gentle light. It was a dance of words and glances, a tentative exploration of what might be if they allowed themselves to believe in the possibility of us once again.

After they were done eating, the leftover bits and pieces were all over the blanket, showing they had a pretty good time. Melanie, ever so neatly, flicked off a crumb from her dress. When Ace's fingers accidentally brushed against hers, she looked up.

"Let's check out the view," he said in a low voice, pulling her up gently.

She went with him, stepping out of the treehouse onto its deck. The night wrapped around them like a dark, cozy blanket, making the stars pop out like sparkles on black cloth. It was like looking up into a box of glitter that went on forever.

"Wow, see that?" Ace pointed to the sky, full of wonder. Melanie followed his hand, her eyes wide as they jumped from one star to another.

"It's always so wild to see this," she whispered back, as if talking any louder would break the spell. "Each star's like its own little piece of a much bigger story."

Ace seemed just as caught up in the moment. "People say stars shine brightest when it's darkest. Makes you think, maybe our rough patches were there so we could see these bright spots clearer."

Melanie thought about that, feeling a mix of hope and reflection. His words made her see him—and their past—in a new light.

"Could be," she agreed, thinking out loud. "It's all about finding our way back to each other, no matter how twisted the road might get."

"Exactly, like we're on some kind of quest for the perfect harmony," Ace added, his face lit up by the starlight. "Or like that story of coming back home after a long time away."

Her laughter joined his, creating a sweet melody under the vast sky.

They stood close, occasionally touching in a reassuring way. Melanie felt a rush of warmth from being near Ace, making the cool air around them feel just right.

"So, what's next for us, Mel?" Ace asked, his voice full of quiet hope.

"We keep going," she said confidently. "Led by faith, hand in hand with love."

"And if we hit a rough patch?" He looked at her, a bit wary of the future.

"Then we'll face it head-on," she said firmly, giving his hand a reassuring squeeze. "We've got God on our side, so there's nothing we can't handle."

Ace laughed softly, pulling her closer. "Looks like we're quite the duo, huh?"

"Sure are," she leaned into him, feeling safe and sound. "It's just like life to turn a mess into a masterpiece."

"Melanie Barnett," Ace said, sounding more serious now, "I can't wait to see where our duets lead us."

"Acer Andreas," Melanie responded, feeling hopeful about what's to come, "I think we're in for something really special."

Looking up at the sky filled with stars, they both felt excited about the future—a future where their love, faith, and forgiveness would be the main themes of their journey together.

Thirteen

Heart of the Community

The day had an almost electric feel to it as Melanie stepped into the cozy, sunlit space of the music studio Ace has built on his property, it had become her home away from home. The walls, lined with framed records and inspirational quotes, seemed to echo with the possibility of what was to come. "Guess what?" she practically sang the words as Ace looked up from tuning a guitar.

"What's up?" Ace asked, his interest piqued by the sparkle in Melanie's eyes.

"I got a call from Harmony Gospel Records. They want me to audition!" Melanie's voice was a mix of excitement and disbelief.

"That's amazing!" Ace's response was immediate and genuine. He set the guitar aside, giving Melanie his full attention. "You're going to knock their socks off."

Melanie laughed, the sound light and joyful. "I hope so. But, Ace, I'm nervous. What if I mess up?"

Ace stood and walked over to her, taking her hands in his. "Mel, you've been preparing for this your whole life. Your voice, your faith, your heart—it's all going to shine through."

The encouragement meant the world to Melanie. They spent hours in the studio, Ace listening patiently as Melanie practiced her set, offering feedback and praise in equal measure.

Melanie was practically bouncing off the walls of her cozy little house, buzzing with a mix of crazy excitement and those jittery pre-show nerves. Today was huge, the kind of day she'd been dreaming about since she was belting out gospel tunes in her church's kiddie choir.

Ace was there, chilling against the counter with his coffee, throwing her amused looks. "Gonna drill a hole in the floor if you keep at it," he joked, his voice all smooth and calm.

Melanie paused, giving him that look. "Well, sorry for the nerves, Mr. Cool. It's not every day I audition for a gospel label," she shot back, her voice a cocktail of pretend annoyance and real butterflies.

"I get it, I do," Ace said, putting his coffee down and coming over. He took her hands, his inked arms a stark contrast to her own. "Listen, Mel, you're ready for this. Your voice? It's something else. It's not just nice to listen to; it moves people, deep down, God has blessed you."

Locking eyes with him, Melanie found the reassurance she needed. "Thanks, Ace. Means a ton, having you believe in me like this."

The drive over to the Harmony Records in the Metro a few hours away felt like a blur of emotions. The place looked intimidating as heck from the outside, but stepping in, Melanie felt right at home. This was her jam, where she was meant to shine.

The audition itself was intense. Melanie threw everything she had into it, all her passion, faith, and dreams. The room was filled with the power of her voice, echoing off the walls and leaving this amazing silence hanging after she finished.

Then came the big moment: the label wanted her. She was over the moon, couldn't believe it. She'd done it, landed a deal to record a gospel album. Elation swept through her, a tidal wave of joy and disbelief. She'd done it.

That evening, still riding that high, she and Ace went over the contract, buzzing with excitement and a bit of good old caution. "We should get my lawyer to check this out, just to make sure everything's kosher," Ace suggested, always looking out for her.

"Definitely," Melanie agreed, her head still spinning. "This is nuts. Like, actual dream-come-true territory."

Ace pulled her in for a hug, his excitement matching hers. "This is just the start, Mel. You're going places."

They laughed and dreamt about the future together, filling the room with hope and plans. Melanie Barnett, the girl with the powerhouse voice from a small town, was on the edge of something huge. And Ace? He was right there with her, every step of the way.

FOURTEEN

Crossroads and Choices

In the days following Melanie's successful audition, Ace couldn't shake a growing sense of unease. It lingered in the background, a shadow amidst their shared happiness. He was in his office, reviewing the final details of the casino sale with his lawyer, when his phone buzzed with a message that sent a chill down his spine.

"Rocco Moretti wants to meet. Says it's urgent," the text from an old contact read. Ace knew then that the shadows of his past were creeping closer than he'd anticipated.

"Who's Rocco Moretti?" his lawyer asked, noticing the change in Ace's demeanor.

"A ghost from my past life," Ace replied, his voice tight. "Looks like he's not ready to let me go just yet."

Rocco Moretti, a name that once commanded respect and fear in the underbelly of the east coast, was the last person Ace wanted entangled in his new life. Moretti, having caught wind of the casino sale, saw an opportunity to expand his influence and was not about to let it slip through his fingers.

Ace arranged to meet Moretti in a nondescript diner on the outskirts of town, a place where deals were made and broken in hushed tones. The meeting was tense, with Moretti making it clear he wanted the casino, and he was willing to go to great lengths to get it.

"I heard you're selling to the Basito's," Moretti said, his voice low and dangerous. "I think it would be better for everyone if it stayed in familiar hands, don't you?"

Ace felt the old instincts kick in, the urge to stand his ground against the threat. "It's not about what's better for everyone. It's about doing what's right, for once."

Moretti leaned back, a sinister smile playing on his lips. "Don't forget where you come from, Ace. People like us, we don't get to walk away clean."

The meeting ended with unspoken threats hanging in the air. Ace drove back to Havencrest, his mind racing with possible repercussions. He knew Moretti wasn't the type to take no for an answer. The thought of Melanie being caught in the crossfire was unbearable.

He found Melanie in the studio, her laughter a beacon of light in his stormy thoughts. Without mentioning Moretti, he wrapped her in a hug, a silent promise to protect her from the shadows encroaching on their happiness.

But as the days passed, the tension grew. Unfamiliar cars lingered a little too long near the community centers, and whispers of Moretti's displeasure reached Ace through the grapevine. He bolstered security around the church, community centers, and their homes, a necessary precaution that weighed heavily on him.

One evening, as he drove her home from a late dinner, Melanie sensed Ace's distraction. "What's on your mind? You've been miles away all night."

Ace debated how much to share, not wanting to alarm her. "Just business stuff, trying to make sure everything goes smoothly with the casino sale."

Melanie turned, taking his hands in hers. "Whatever it is, we'll face it together. You're not alone in this, Ace."

Her words, filled with faith and courage, reminded Ace of what he was fighting for. "Together," he echoed, drawing strength from her presence.

As they continued their drive, the starry sky above Havencrest seemed to mock the darkness lurking in the corners of Ace's world. He realized then that no matter how far he had come, the shadows of his past would always threaten to disrupt the harmony he'd found. But with Melanie by his side, perhaps there was hope for a brighter future, one where shadows had no place to hide.

FIFTEEN

Seeds of a New Beginning

Melanie stood on the porch of her immaculately maintained home, her heart pounding a steady rhythm in sync with the gentle breeze that rustled through the night air. The delicate blue chiffon of her dress danced at her ankles as she waited, her large brown eyes reflecting the heavens transitioning from twilight to the deep blue of evening. Following a day spent in thoughtful prayer and preparation, she was ready to face the night—and the man who would soon arrive.

The distant purr of an engine signaled his approach before a sleek black sedan slid into view. Ace stepped out, looking every bit the masculine man who had walked straight off the pages of a high-end fashion magazine. His suit was impeccably tailored, accentuating his muscular physique and strong jawline. As he approached, Melanie couldn't help but recall the many times they had attended church together—Sunday mornings when opening doors was reserved for men of faith and character.

"Melanie," Ace began, his honey-colored eyes softening as they took her in, "you look stunning."

His gaze lingered on her in awe. Her hair was cascading in soft waves over her shoulders; her makeup, enhancing her natural beauty; and her smile seemed to reflect her heart, filled with love for both Ace and the Lord.

"Thank you, Ace," she replied, her voice steady, betraying none of the swirling emotions within her. "You clean up quite nicely yourself."

The corners of his mouth lifted into that familiar cocky grin—a silent reminder of their shared past and the chasm that had lay between them in the past. They descended the porch steps together, and as he opened the car door for her, she couldn't help but remember their days as young lovers seeking guidance from God's word through regular church attendance.

The drive was a quiet symphony of city sounds muffled by the luxury of the car's interior. Ace's hand occasionally brushed against the gear shift in a way that drew Melanie's attention to the tattoos peeking out from under his shirt cuffs—silent verses of a life he struggled to reconcile with his own convictions.

They pulled up to "Andreas" —the Italian restaurant that was more than just a name on a sign; it was a legacy steeped in tradition and family values. The facade held an old-world charm that belied the modern empire it fronted. As they entered the establishment, Melanie took a deep breath, steadying herself for the evening ahead—an encounter that would challenge both their faith and love for one another.

The maître d' welcomed them with a reverence that bordered on deferential, further solidifying Ace's status. As they followed him through the dining room, Melanie couldn't help but feel the weight of the unseen eyes upon them—the congregation of Ace's world judging her suitability.

Ace's hand at the small of her back was both an anchor and a temptation, a touch that spoke of protection yet promised so much more. Melanie allowed herself this dance of proximity, aware of the fine line she treaded between her desires and her devotion.

"Your father certainly knows how to create an atmosphere," Melanie observed, her tone light, though her insides were a tangle of nerves and prayers.

"Wait until you try the food," Ace replied, his confidence in this place, in his family, shining through like the flickering candles that adorned each table.

Ace's hand guided Melanie past the labyrinth of linen-draped tables, each a tiny island adrift in the soft glow of candlelight. The melody of a violin solo weaved through the air, harmonizing with the subdued chatter and clinking of fine china—an orchestrated symphony of dining elegance.

"Here we are," Ace announced as they arrived at their secluded haven, tucked away from the prying eyes of the world outside their intimate circle. The table, set for five, was an enclave of privacy framed by the rich velvet drapes that absorbed the murmurs of the restaurant.

"Perfect," Melanie breathed out, allowing herself to be enveloped by the alcove's warmth—a stark contrast to the chill of apprehension that had accompanied her thus far.

"Only the best for you," Ace said, his voice a low baritone that resonated with sincerity.

He pulled out a chair for her, a gesture so fluid and practiced it could have been part of a dance. As she sat, the fabric of her dress whispered against the cushioned seat, a tactile symphony that underscored her every move.

"Thank you," she replied, her gaze lifting to meet his. There was a reverence in his eyes, a depth that seemed to see beyond her external composure to the trepidation that fluttered like a delicate butterfly within her chest.

As Ace took his place opposite her, Melanie glanced around the corner of their sanctuary and caught sight of Ace's family walking toward them.

"Melanie, great to see you again," Jax greeted, his voice a bass note that complemented the violin's sweet lament.

"Jax, always a pleasure," Melanie responded, her smile genuine but tinged with the nervous awareness of being under the scrutiny of Ace's kin.

Tre, the embodiment of carefree charm, flashed a grin that crinkled the corners of his eyes—eyes so similar to Ace's yet filled with a mirth that seemed untouched by the shadows of their shared history.

"Hey, Mel. You look amazing tonight," Tre chimed in, his words carrying the easy cadence of a playful melody.

"Thank you, Tre. It's good to see you both," she returned, her tone light, belying the inner chorus of doubts that reverberated in her mind.

A moment of silence settled over them, comfortable yet charged with unspoken understanding. Melanie reached for the crystal glass before her, the cool touch of the stem grounding her as she allowed herself a sip of water, the liquid clear and pure—a symbol of the clarity she sought amidst the complexities of her heart.

Ace watched her, his expression one of open admiration. . Then walking toward the table was none other than Thomas Andreas, Ace's father - a man whose features appeared chiseled from granite, yet whose demeanor evinced a quiet grace. He approached the table with the gravity of a man accustomed to commanding attention. He moved with purpose, his dark eyes settling on Melanie as he arrived.

"Melanie," Thomas greeted with an outstretched hand, "It's wonderful to see you beyond the confines of our beloved church."

"Mr. Andreas, the pleasure is all mine," Melanie replied, her voice steady despite the fluttering in her chest. His handshake was firm, yet there was warmth there—a quiet acknowledgment of her significance in Ace's life.

"Please, call me Thomas," he said, pulling out a chair and taking his seat at the head of the table. The dim light played across his features, softening the hard edges of his face.

"Thomas," she acquiesced, nodding respectfully. She noted the way his smile reached his eyes, it was clear this was more than him just making an effort for Ace's sake. She appreciated the gesture, knowing well the complexities of reconciling faith with the shadows of one's past.

Ace cleared his throat gently, a reverberating sound that seemed to harmonize with the soft music floating through the air, drawing Melanie's attention back to the present moment. He stood up, his tall frame casting a protective shadow over her as he reached out a hand to help her stand beside him.

"Family," he began, his voice rich with an emotion that didn't need to be named, "I want you to officially meet Melanie Barnett."

Melanie felt Ace's gaze upon her, warm like sunlight dappling through stained glass windows on a Sunday morning. She adjusted the hem of her dress—a modest navy blue that complemented her curves and echoed the sincerity of her faith.

"This is the woman who has captured my heart," Ace continued, the pride in his voice resonating in the intimate space. "The one I love."

"Welcome back, Melanie," Jax said, standing to envelop her in a bear hug that was surprisingly gentle for a man of his stature. His laughter rumbled through her, and she felt the tension ease from her shoulders.

"Thank you, Jax," she replied, her smile genuine as she settled back into her seat. Her eyes danced with merriment, reflecting the playful twinkle in Ace's honey-colored irises.

As if summoned by Thomas's arrival, a waiter appeared, poised to take their orders. The soft clinking of cutlery against fine china provided a delicate soundtrack to the unfolding moment.

"May I start with your order, sir?" the waiter inquired, directing his attention to Thomas first.

"Ah, yes," Thomas began, but it was Ace who caught the waiter's gaze next, a silent overture to let him lead this particular dance.

"Actually, I'll take care of it," Ace interjected smoothly, his voice carrying the confident timbre of a man who knew exactly what he wanted. "Melanie will have the fettucine alla vodka, please. And make sure it's with the sun-dried tomatoes on top, just like she likes."

Melanie felt a rush of warmth at the mention of her favorite, a dish tied to memories of simpler times. How had he remembered? Her heart sang a quiet note of gratitude, the melody intertwining with the chords of her rekindled feelings.

"Still remembering the little things, huh?" she remarked, her lips curving into an appreciative smile.

"Always," Ace replied, locking eyes with her. The intensity in his gaze was a silent vow, echoing through the chambers of her heart like a solemn hymn.

"Very well," the waiter said, scribbling down the order before turning to the others.

As the waiter continued around the table, Melanie's mind hummed with thoughts, the lyrics of her future writing themselves in her soul. Sitting here among the Andreas men, with their complicated histories and hopeful futures, she felt a harmony building—a composition of acceptance, understanding, and the tentative beginnings of familial love.

Sixteen

The Fabric of Forgiveness

Thomas watched her, his eyes reflecting a respect that bordered on admiration. For a brief moment, the music of possibility filled the space between them, a silent prayer that even in a world marred by discord and temptation, faith and love could still find a place to flourish.

Melanie's fork twirled the fettuccine, capturing a perfect bite as laughter spilled from Jax's lips, filling the room like a joyful melody. "And then," he said with a grin that echoed his brother's, "Ace thought he could outdo me on the motorcycle. Ended up in a rosebush instead of at the finish line."

"Hey now, those thorns were tactical defense," Ace interjected, his playful retort a dance of light across Melanie's heartstrings.

"Defense? More like divine intervention to keep your ego in check," Tre chimed in, raising his glass in mock salute.

Melanie chuckled, her laughter harmonizing with the Andreas brothers'. The warm glow of shared memories washed over her, infusing the private corner with an almost sacred intimacy. Her gaze shifted to Ace, whose honey-colored eyes remained fixed on her, a silent sonnet of adoration that resonated deep within her soul.

"Your brothers have quite the archive of stories, Ace," she said, her voice a tender note amidst the symphony of familial banter.

"Only because I provide them with such excellent material," Ace replied, his cocky grin softened by the tenderness in his eyes.

She sipped her wine, the rich flavor mingling with the sweetness of the moment. As their meal progressed, the stories wove a tapestry of life's crescendos and diminuendos, each tale a testament to the family's bond.

"Remember when Dad took us fishing?" Ace said, turning to his brothers. "I've never seen anyone pray for patience as much as he did that day."

"Patience and a miracle to catch anything with you scaring all the fish away," Jax added, earning a chorus of laughs.

"Miracles happened often around here, it seems," Melanie remarked, her mind reflecting on the subtle miracles of grace and forgiveness that had transformed her own relationship with Ace.

"Indeed they do," Thomas said, his voice carrying the weight of wisdom and experience. "The Lord works in mysterious ways, especially within families."

Ace's hand brushed against hers briefly under the table—a fleeting caress, but enough to send a shiver through her. She caught him watching her again, his gaze like a fervent prayer, willing her to understand the depth of his emotion without words.

Their eyes locked, and for a moment, the world around them muted into a hushed reverence. The clinking of cutlery, the whispers of conversation, the soft music playing—it all faded into a backdrop for the silent confession unfolding between them.

In that gaze, Melanie saw the Ace who had captured her heart so many years ago, the boy who had grown into a man shaped by trials and redemption. Here he was, laying bare the tender vulnerability beneath his tough exterior. And she knew, without a shadow of doubt, that his love was as unwavering as her faith.

"Melanie," Ace finally broke the silence, his voice a gentle whisper that only she could hear, "you are the song my heart has always known, the melody that leads me home."

Her response was a smile, radiant and full of the hope that encircled them—a hope that promised second chances and whispered of future harmonies yet to be composed.

The last notes of a violin's serenade lingered in the air like the sweet aroma of tiramisu, which now sat half-eaten between Melanie and Ace. The evening had unfolded like a carefully composed cantata, each movement more enchanting than the last. Melanie's heart thrummed with a mixture of anticipation and nostalgia as the final course concluded, the taste of coffee and cocoa dusting her palate.

Ace's hand, warm and steady, found Melanie's atop the white linen tablecloth. His fingers interlaced with hers, a silent plea for connection that echoed louder than any spoken word. Her skin tingled at the contact, an electric current leaping from his touch to the very core of her being. His eyes, those honey-hued orbs, held a softness she hadn't seen in years, their usual defiance replaced with something far more formidable—vulnerability.

"Melanie," he began, his voice barely rising above the hush of intimate conversations surrounding them. "I've been walking down a long road to get here—a road paved with mistakes and lessons hard-learned."

She watched, entranced, as Ace's thumb gently caressed the back of her hand, a metronome keeping time with his confession. A waiter passed by, refilling their water glasses, but the world outside their bubble might as well have dissolved into oblivion.

"Since we parted ways," Ace continued, "I've been searching for something... someone who could make me feel whole again. And I realized, it's always been you, Mel." His voice cracked, but he pressed on, "You are the grace note in my life—the beauty in a composition that was once only chaos."

Melanie felt her breath catch in her throat, her own pulse drumming an erratic rhythm against her ribs. She had dreamt of this moment, prayed for it in quiet whispers during choir practice, when her voice soared and dipped with the lilting praises of the gospel hymns. Yet here, now, it was unfolding more beautifully than she could have ever imagined.

"Your faith, your strength," Ace said, "they inspire me. They remind me that there's still good in this world, and it's worth fighting for. You've changed me, Melanie, for the better."

A single tear escaped, gliding down Melanie's cheek like a raindrop on the windowpane of a sanctuary. It wasn't sadness that brought forth the tear, but rather a profound recognition of the truth in his words. She knew Ace's past, the shadows that clung to him, but here he was before her, a man reborn through love and humility.

"Every day since we've reconnected has been a step closer to redemption," he spoke with earnest intensity. "I want to build a life with you, one filled with love and laughter...and yes, even the occasional off-key note, because perfection isn't real. But we... we could be something extraordinary."

Their gazes remained locked, two souls entwined in a duet of longing and hope. The melody of their past played softly between them, but it was the uncharted symphony of their future that danced within Melanie's mind. She squeezed his hand in return, a nonverbal chorus of shared dreams and acceptance.

"Melanie," Ace began, his voice barely above a whisper yet carrying the weight of years and transformation. "I once thought I knew what it meant to live fiercely—to grab hold of life with both hands. But you," he paused, dropping to one knee, an act of surrender and strength, "you taught me that true courage is found in the gentleness of a shared prayer, in the quiet moments of reflection."

The restaurant seemed to stand still, holding its breath as Ace reached into his pocket. The ring he produced glimmered like a beacon—a circle of trust and eternity. It was a beautiful paradox, simple yet intricate, much like the faith they both cherished.

"Will you marry me?" he asked, the ring extended towards her like an offering at the altar of their future.

Melanie's breath hitched, her heart pounding a rhythm that resonated with the divine symphony she'd always believed in. A single tear welled up, brimming with the essence of every psalm of joy she'd ever sung. She gazed at the ring, seeing in its facets the reflection of a church aisle, the echo of wedding bells, and the promise of a love that could move mountains.

"Yes," she breathed out, her voice a melody of acceptance and adoration. "Yes, Ace, I will marry you." Her hands reached for his, fingers intertwining in a dance of destiny.

As he slipped the ring onto her finger, a perfect fit, Melanie felt a surge of gratitude for the serendipitous turn that had led them back to each other. In this room, surrounded by the warmth of family and the resonance of soft music, her spirit soared on the wings of newfound hope.

Ace rose, enveloping her in an embrace that spoke volumes more than any sermon or scripture. In his hold, she understood the depth of redemption, the reality of grace that forgave all past transgressions.

The din of clinking glasses and silverware faded into a hushed reverence as Ace's lips met Melanie's in a kiss that was both a pledge and a prayer. It was the crescendo of their symphony, an intimate harmony that resonated through the private alcove and soon spread like a jubilant chorus throughout the restaurant.

"Forever starts now," Ace whispered against her lips, his voice barely audible over the rising swell of cheers.

Melanie opened her eyes to the sight of patrons standing, their applause rolling like thunderous waves upon the shore of her heart. Her gaze swept across the room, catching the joyous faces of Ace's brothers, Jax and Tre, who whistled with brotherly pride. Thomas Andreas beamed, his approval shining like a benediction.

"They're celebrating us?," Melanie asked, her voice a lilting mixture of awe and gratitude.

"Because they see what I see—the most incredible woman in the world agreeing to be my wife." Ace's eyes twinkled, his cocky grin emerging for a fleeting moment before it softened into something more profound.

Melanie laughed, a sound as clear and sweet as the crystal goblets raised in their honor. The sensation of his hands on her back, strong and steady, anchored her amidst the waves of adulation. She leaned into him, her own hands exploring the contours of his suit—a fabric that could not constrain the wild heart beating beneath.

"Let's give them a reason to keep cheering." Ace's words were a tease, but his intent was clear as he drew her in once more.

Their second kiss was a testament to the journey they'd embarked upon—a path fraught with trials and temptations yet cleared by the strength of their faith and love. Melanie's mind soared, each cheer a note in the anthem of their redemption. The melodies of past heartaches faded, replaced by a song of hope and commitment that she had longed to sing.

"God's grace," she thought, her spirit alight with the truth of the words. They were a covenant, not just between herself and Ace, but with their shared beliefs, their intertwined futures.

SEVENTEEN

Echoes of Transformation

Melanie's laughter bubbled through Ace's cozy living room, a stark contrast to the crackling fire casting a warm glow. She shifted on the couch, facing him with excitement evident in her sparkling eyes.

"Guess what? Mom's flight is all set, she'll be getting in the Thursday before the wedding and staying with my aunt at this little bed & breakfast they've both been raving about!" Melanie's hands gestured animatedly, brimming with joy. "She's as hyped as we are about this little mini reunion."

Ace grinned, relaxed against the couch with an arm casually draped over it. "Can't wait to see her again in person, it's been too long," he said sincerely, acknowledging the significance her seeing the man he had become versus the little boy who abandoned her daughter. Being welcomed back into Melanie's family meant more than just a simple introduction; it symbolized the acceptance he craved since leaving his past behind.

"Really?" Melanie searched his face for reassurance, finding it in his unwavering nod.

"Absolutely." Ace's voice carried weight, emphasizing the importance of this step. "Being part of your family... it's everything to me."

"You know, your past doesn't faze her," Melanie whispered, intertwining her fingers with his. Her touch conveyed warmth and forgiveness, embodying the faith she had in him. "Redemption is something she believes in as much as I do."

"I've got two strong women on my side then," Ace replied softly, his thumb tracing comforting circles over her hand.

"Make that three," Melanie corrected playfully. "Aunt Rosa will make sure you remember she's rooting for you too."

A chuckle escaped Ace, blending with the soothing crackles of the fire. "Three against one? Those odds, even I wouldn't bet against."

Melanie squeezed his hand tighter, her heart syncing with the hopeful cadence of their intertwined future. "We're all in this together, Ace. You're not fighting alone anymore."

The weight of her words settled upon him, a comforting blanket woven from threads of loyalty and love. He turned to her, his amber eyes reflecting the fire's glow and the solemn vow within them. "I'll be the man you all believe I can be. For you, for them... for us."

Her gaze didn't waver, reading the symphony of promises etched in his expression. “I know you will, Ace. You've already shown me the strength of your heart.”

As the flames whispered secrets of warmth and endurance, two souls sat in an embrace of quiet understanding, the resonance of their shared dreams harmonizing with the humble crackle of firewood. In this house of second chances, where the shadows of former animosities gave way to the light of blossoming love, Ace and Melanie beheld the dawn of a new chapter—a melody composed by divine grace and the resilience of the human spirit.

The flickering glow of the fire painted a dance of red and gold upon the walls as Melanie and Ace sat, nestled into the corner of the plush couch. The movie's credits rolled silently on the screen before them, its story concluded but theirs still unfolding. Melanie's gaze lingered momentarily on the actors taking their final bow before turning towards Ace, her eyes alight with a different kind of anticipation.

"Imagine," she began softly, tracing a pattern on his tattooed forearm, "when it's us up there—well, not on a screen, but...

you know, in the spotlight, surrounded by our loved ones, stepping into the future together."

Ace shifted, leaning in closer to her, his tough exterior softening under her touch. "You know," he started, a hint of playfulness in his deep voice, "have you ever thought about how many little mini-us's we'd want running around?"

Melanie's heart skipped a beat at the unexpected question, a mix of excitement and nerves swirling inside her. "Kids," she murmured, the idea blooming like a favorite tune in her mind. "I've always pictured having our own mini choir."

A mischievous grin tugged at Ace's lips. "A choir, huh? How many tiny voices are we talking about here?"

"Maybe three or four," she replied with a chuckle, blending laughter with their serious chat. "Enough to fill our place with chaos and love songs."

"Three or four it is then," he laughed deeply, the sound mingling with the crackling fire. Leaning forward, elbows on his knees, he pondered their future filled with little ones making noise. "I love that idea," he confessed sincerely. "A house bursting with life, music... and most importantly, love."

"Really?" Melanie studied him for a moment before finding honesty shining in his eyes.

"Absolutely." Ace turned back to her with earnestness. "You've shown me there's more to life than just surviving—it's about creating something beautiful together. Our family will be my greatest achievement and ministry."

"I agree," she breathed out softly, feeling their dreams aligning perfectly. "But we'll need a strong base first—something built on faith and grace."

"We're already building that with Christ," Ace whispered firmly, squeezing her hand gently as if sealing the promise between them. "Piece by piece, prayer by prayer. A safe haven where our future kids can thrive knowing they're cherished and belong."

His thumb brushed against her skin tenderly as if pledging protection and comfort. Melanie smiled at Ace as she envisioned their shared future. Ace lifted their clasped hands to his lips planting a gentle kiss on hers.

Melanie stood up from the couch, her figure casting a soft shadow in the flickering firelight. She pulled her sweater closer around her as the room cooled without Ace's presence. The crackling fire provided warmth, contrasting with the uncertainty lingering in Melanie's mind.

"The next month is going to be crazy," she said, her voice a melody against the dying embers' hum. "It feels surreal that it's almost here." She walked towards the hallway, her steps barely audible on the hardwood floor. Ace observed her, his inner conflict evident on his face. He rose and followed her to the guest room doorway, where the promise of a new day lay as real as the Bible on the nightstand.

"It's all falling into place, Mel. " Turning to him, Melanie's expressive eyes shimmered in the room's golden light, full of dreams waiting to unfold.

"Do you think we're really prepared for this?" Her question hung vulnerably in the air.

"We're more than ready," Ace replied confidently.

"Our home will be bursting with love and God, that's what's more important." She twirled a strand of hair around her finger, lost in thought.

"Yes. God, love, and children with your spirit and my..." Ace paused briefly before continuing, "...determination."

"Stubbornness?" Melanie teased with a playful smile.

"Let's call it determination," he countered with a hint of cockiness. "They'll be unstoppable."

Ace turned to Melanie, his gaze lingering on her with a tenderness that belied his rugged exterior. "I love you, Mel," he said, his voice carrying the weight of his commitment. "More than I ever thought possible."

Melanie's heart felt full, swelling with a melody of emotion as she looked into his honey-colored eyes. Each word he spoke was a note in the symphony of their future, every sentence a vow. "And I love you, Ace," she whispered back, her hands finding his with a natural grace.

"Whatever it takes, whatever you need, I'm here." His thumb traced soft circles on the back of her hand. "I'll be the man who earns your trust every day, the one who walks beside you in faith and love."

She could see it—the sincerity, the fierce determination etched in the lines of his face, the way his eyes seemed to search her soul for confirmation. It was more than just words; it was the pledge of a reformed spirit.

Their lips met in a kiss that seared far deeper than the heat from the hearth. It was a passionate affirmation of all they had overcome, a heated blend of past regrets and present desires. Melanie's mind raced with the intensity of the moment, her pulse thrumming in time with the crackle of the fire.

But as the fervor grew, Ace's resolve wavered. He felt the old temptations clawing at the edges of his newfound control, the familiar urge to claim, to dominate, rising within him. With a strength that came from somewhere divine, he gently pulled away, his breath ragged, his restraint evident in the tightness of his jaw.

"Mel," he began, steadying himself, "the guest room is ready for you. I want nothing more than to wake up knowing you're safe here, but I respect you too much to rush what's sacred between us."

Her cheeks were flushed, her breathing uneven, but in her eyes, he saw understanding, a reflection of their mutual promise to honor the boundaries of their beliefs.

"I can't wait to see you in the morning," he added, a smile tugging at the corner of his mouth—a smile that told her he was hers completely, unreservedly, in body, heart, and soul.

As she stood, her fingers lingered briefly on his, the simple touch speaking volumes of shared anticipation. The night air held the whispers of their devotion, a song of patience and passion, waiting to be fulfilled in the light of a new day.

As Melanie disappeared into the guest room and closed the door behind her, she glanced back at Ace before whispering softly, "Goodnight."

"Sweet dreams, future Mrs. Andreas," Ace responded proudly and lovingly as she settled in for the night. The door sealed shut behind her as Melanie leaned against it briefly, savoring what lay ahead. Their wedding day loomed near—a dawn of fresh beginnings filled with silent promises and cherished vows beating within her heart.

Eighteen

The Dance of Destiny

The Andreas' family living room exuded a blend of sophistication and warmth, with its spacious layout and plush, modern furniture creating a cozy atmosphere for the family gathering. Ace lounged against the sleek marble fireplace, his demeanor relaxed yet attentive. Excitement crackled in the air as they finalized the details of the casino deal.

"Once the Basito Family gives their approval, it's a done deal," Jax remarked in his reassuring bass voice, a hint of relief evident in his tone.

"No more constantly looking over your shoulder."

"Freedom," Ace whispered softly to himself, savoring the unfamiliar taste of the word on his lips like a newfound melody. It was a tune he never imagined he'd get to sing.

"Prayerfully," Thomas chimed in gravely, locking eyes with Ace, silently acknowledging their shared struggles and unspoken prayers for redemption and peace. A bond forged through battles fought and scars hidden beneath well-tailored shirts. Surveying their expressions—etched with relief and lingering worry—Ace felt the grip of his past life loosening. The days where fear secured respect seemed distant compared to the tranquility, he now sought with Melanie's unwavering faith embracing him. The jarring ring of Thomas' phone shattered the moment abruptly. All eyes darted to him as he answered, a sudden pallor washing over his face like a ghostly veil stealing color away. Dread coiled in Ace's chest at once familiar and unwelcome.

"Who is it?" Jax's concern resonated deeply in his baritone voice. "They're threatening Melanie... put her on watch," Thomas muttered after hanging up, his hand trembling imperceptibly as he set down the phone. "It's from the Moretti's."

"Heaven help us," Jax breathed out quietly, barely audible amidst Ace's rushing pulse.

"Melanie? We knew this might happen." Tre's admission hung heavily in the air. A suffocating silence settled over the room, each breath laden with unease. The innocuous phone now sat ominously on the table—a bearer of news that reverberated through them like an ominous chord. Jax locked eyes with Tre, wordlessly affirming solidarity born from shared trials—a vow unspoken but understood: they would confront this threat together.

"Melanie..." Tre began again, worry tinging his rumbling voice unmistakably.

"She's at risk because of us," Jax finished grimly, bracing himself against the sofa as if preparing for impact. Ace clenched his fists where he stood; tension etched into every line of his body.

With each measured breath came a silent prayer and a resolute promise: "We won't let anything happen to her," he declared firmly, masking inner turmoil beneath a composed facade.

"You know what we're up against," Jax cautioned somberly.

"Melanie doesn't deserve this," Tre paced restlessly now, mirroring an unsettled melody searching for harmony.

"I won't let anything happen to her," Ace asserted before turning away to gaze at the family Bible resting prominently on the mantel—a worn testament to years past that anchored him with its quiet strength.

"Halting your wedding won't change their minds," Jax pointed out sternly, arms crossed defensively across his chest.

"It may not," Ace conceded as frustration simmered beneath his calm exterior; running a hand through his hair in discordant agitation. "But I can't walk her down that aisle knowing she's targeted."

"Have faith in God's plan for you both," Tre interjected gently into the heavy atmosphere, attempting to inject hope into shadows looming large around them. Meeting Tre's gaze squarely, Ace found not just his usual carefree spirit but also an unwavering ally.

"So, what are we going to do about this?" Tre asked, arms folded over his chest.

Melanie Brown entered the Andreas' home, a binder filled with vibrant swatches in hand. The usually lively atmosphere was replaced by an unsettling tension. Ace's warm eyes, typically sparkling with mischief, now held a clouded gaze as he greeted her.

"Hey, Melanie," Ace's voice carried a weight of concern that wasn't lost on her.

"Hi, everyone," Melanie attempted to lighten the mood, displaying her wedding planner. "Ready to tackle this?"

Silent exchanges passed between the family members, their expressions inscrutable. Sensing the charged atmosphere, Melanie felt a faint tremor of unease creeping in. The air crackled with unspoken words.

Ace gestured towards the hallway, his urgency palpable. "Can we talk?"

Following him to a study lined with books and memories of his family's past, Melanie's heart quickened. The scent of leather and aged paper enveloped her as Ace closed the door behind them with deliberate care.

"Is something wrong?" Melanie's fingers sought comfort in tracing a hymnal's spine on the shelf amidst uncertainty.

"There's been a threat against you," Ace confessed, his distress evident in every word. "Because of my past."

Fear gripped her heart at the revelation but Melanie refused to falter. Her faith stood firm against the storm brewing within her.

"Should we postpone the wedding?" she asked calmly despite the chaos swirling inside her.

"No," Ace's resolve was unwavering. "I won't let them ruin our future."

Their eyes met in silent understanding; a promise of unity forged in adversity. Hand in hand, they returned to face whatever challenges lay ahead—Melanie's faith and music harmonizing within her like an unwavering melody of hope.

Melanie's reflection quivered in the polished surface of the dining table, her brown eyes ballooning with an awareness that splintered the fragile calm. The air was charged, a symphony of tension played on the faces of the Andreas family, each note of concern etched upon their brows. Yet, as the gravity of the threat sank its teeth into the room, Melanie's spine straightened, her faith a shield against the encroaching fear.

"We can't back down," she declared, her voice rising with determination. "We need to bring their illegal activities to light—expose the Moretti's for who they really are."

Ace observed her, his honey-colored eyes filled with admiration. "Mel, it's risky. I can't bear the thought of you—"

"Being scared doesn't mean we lack faith, Ace," she interrupted gently. Her hand stretched across the table, brushing lightly over his clenched fist. "It's about trusting God despite our fears. We have to tackle this together."

Jax interjected with a throat clearing, grounding the conversation with his deep voice. "She's right. But we have to be smart—avoid getting caught in the crossfire and gather solid evidence."

Tre leaned back in his chair, playing with a pen as he contemplated. "All that dirty money must be flowing through a vein we can tap without risking too much."

"Surveillance," Ace pondered aloud, his brow furrowed in thought. "We could track their movements and transactions—"

Melanie chimed in, her thoughts aligning with his strategy. "But without diving into the shadows ourselves."

Jax suggested following financial trails but emphasized the need for an expert to sift through records discreetly. Tre proposed having an insider who could gather information without raising suspicion. Ace acknowledged these ideas, tapping on the tabletop in rhythm with his racing heart as he mulled over equipment and expertise requirements.

"Faith," Melanie whispered softly to herself, fighting off doubts by holding onto scriptures that fortified her spirit.

'For God has not given us a spirit of fear...' Ace echoed her sentiment, their unspoken connection deepening with shared understanding.

Jax redirected their focus to outlining steps and preparing for potential risks while emphasizing tight communication channels within the family circle only.

As they geared up for action against the Moretti family's threats looming like storm clouds overhead in the Andreas family home, Ace stood tall—his gaze scanning familiar walls heavy with history and secrets waiting to be unraveled.

"We need intel from the streets and a reliable mole," Ace declared decisively, breaking the tense silence hanging in the air.

"Who?" Jax inquired cautiously.

"Danny," Ace responded confidently, his voice carrying both weariness and hope born from experience.

"Can he be trusted?" Tre interjected sharply.

"Absolutely," Ace affirmed. Melanie watched him, her eyes reflecting the unwavering confidence she held in Ace's judgment.

Ace's tattooed fingers, calloused from past fights, dialed Danny's number, each beep a staccato against the muted apprehension in the room.

"Danny here," Danny's voice came through the line, smooth as a jazz solo on a sultry night.

"Danny, it's Ace."

"Acer Andreas, as I live and breathe." Danny's voice lowered. "What's up my guy – thought you'd left the life."

"I have… But I've hit a snag with the Moretti's." Ace kept his words clipped, conscious of prying digital ears.

"Say no more, brother. You thinking' what I'm thinkin'?"

"Information," Ace said. "Quietly."

"Understood. The less noise, the better," Danny assured him. "We dance this waltz with caution, Ace. You know how these devils play."

"Keep to the shadows, Danny," Ace instructed. "And pray."

"Always do," Danny replied before ending the call.

Ace slipped the phone back into his pocket, turning to face the anxious faces of his family. "Danny's in. He'll gather what we can use to shine a light on the Moretti's dark deeds."

"Good," Melanie breathed, her voice a soothing melody amid the cacophony of worry. "We move forward then."

"Exactly," Ace agreed, his heart echoing the sentiment. "We're not just fighting for the casino sale or even for ourselves. We're in this to protect the future—our love is stronger than any threat they throw at us."

Jax nodded, a resolute beat in his step as he moved to check the security systems. Tre followed suit, his mind already orchestrating countermeasures. Melanie stepped closer to Ace, her hand finding his, their fingers intertwining like woven chords in a divine composition.

"Remember what you told me once?" Melanie whispered, her voice barely audible above the whispering shadows. "That every mafia man has two lives—the one before he finds faith and the one after."

Ace's pulse thrummed in his veins, a reminder of the life he yearned to leave behind. "I remember," he said, feeling the resonance of their joined hands like a vow.

"Then let's make sure the Moretti's only see the man of God you are today," she urged, her eyes alight with the fire of shared conviction. "Not the ghost of the past."

"Melanie," he began, his voice softened by the depth of his emotion, "I..."

She stood, closing the distance between them, placing a gentle hand on his tattooed forearm. "You don't have to say it, Ace. I know."

He enveloped her hand in his, searching her face for any sign of hesitation. There was none. Only certainty and courage.

Ace's eyes locked onto hers, a silent question lingering between them. "Melanie— I love you so much Mel," he murmured, his breath mingling with hers.

"I love you too," she affirmed.

Their lips met in a kiss that was both a promise and a prayer, a momentary reprieve from the battle ahead. They parted, their eyes still locked in a silent vow that no matter the outcome, their love would endure, harmonized by the divine composer of their fate.

The town had quieted down, the warm glow of streetlights stretching long shadows over the sidewalks. Melanie found herself at Ace's doorstep, her heart beating a nervous tune in the hushed surroundings.

"Remember," Ace's voice was soft yet resolute, "stick with Vic or Ramone. I'll likely be away for about a few days; take notes for me at church."

He motioned towards the discreetly positioned men guarding her house, emphasizing the seriousness of the situation. "You can use my room, Sam can take the guest room, and remember the cleaner comes on Tuesday."

Melanie nodded firmly, her lips forming a tight line. "Got it," she replied, glancing past Ace to the security detail he had arranged. She was used to seeing them in cars sitting outside whenever she went, but this was different... more obvious… intrusive.

Their vigilant presence offered some solace despite their stoic expressions. Ace reached out and gently tucked a loose curl behind Melanie's ear, his touch tender beneath his tough exterior.

"I'll make sure you and Sam are safe."

"Sam's already unpacking," Melanie assured him, gesturing towards her friend who was in the guest room making herself at home. She met Ace's gaze under the soft porch light that bathed them in a warm glow. "We'll be okay. You've made sure of that."

"Good." Ace studied her face for a moment before finding reassurance in her determined look. "I'll be back soon. Just... keep me in your prayers and your heart."

"Always," she whispered back, their connection momentarily overpowering any impending danger.

As Ace retreated into the darkness, Melanie watched him go before closing and locking the door behind him, creating a barrier from the outside world. Inside, she joined Sam in the living room with measured steps on the hardwood floor echoing her racing heartbeat. Sam sat casually on the couch with her phone in hand.

"Everything ready?" Sam asked without looking up, her voice steady amidst Melanie's inner turmoil.

"Security's all set," Melanie confirmed as she settled beside her friend on the couch. The concealed recorder hidden under her blouse felt cold against her skin.

"We're like spies in an action movie," Sam teased lightly with a smirk playing on her lips.

"Yeah, except our lives are part of this script," Melanie quipped back weakly, trying to inject humor into their tense situation but falling short.

"Hey," Sam put down her phone and turned to face Melanie with a serious expression now replacing any trace of playfulness. "Are you sure about this? About him?"

Melanie hesitated briefly before nodding resolutely. "Yes. His love... it soothes my soul like music calming a storm within me. And our faith is stronger than any threat from Moretti."

"Then let's pray and believe that melody becomes our victory anthem," Sam declared with newfound determination that resonated with Melanie's resolve.

Glancing at the closed door once more - feeling both apprehension and conviction - Melanie murmured to herself and to Sam alike: "God will guide us through this storm."

"He will," Sam affirmed as they sat side by side like guardians facing unseen perils ahead armed only with their faith, love, and unwavering resolve set to a contemporary beat.

Nineteen

A Symphony of Souls

The night engulfs the decrepit warehouse like a thick, velvet cloak, its shadows swirling with an air of foreboding. Inside, a solitary bulb hangs from the ceiling, suspended by a single cable. It swings lazily, as if moved by the breath of hidden specters. Its feeble glow casts a meager circle of light, struggling to reach the four men gathered below.

Ace's eyes, the color of aged whiskey, scan the rough interior, taking in the graffiti that adorns the walls. Each spray-painted stroke tells a tale of forgotten deals and shattered allegiances, bleeding onto the concrete in vibrant hues.

"The place gives me the creeps," Tre mutters, his voice echoing faintly in the cavernous space.

"Focus," Jax commands with a low rumble, his imposing figure silhouetted against the dim light. "We're not here for renovations."

Restlessness consumes Ace, causing his steps to echo throughout the concrete floor. Each footfall is a steady beat, like a metronome counting down to an inevitable moment. Tension crackles in the air, burdened by decisions yet to be made. He can almost hear a distant hum of a song lingering on the fringes of my consciousness—a reminder of the path he once walked, now obscured by the choices he's made.

"Alright, Danny," Ace's voice slices through the silence, sharp and direct.

Danny shifts uneasily, his face flickering as he leans into the light. Shadows dance across his features like phantoms writhing in torment. "The Moretti's are growing bolder," he begins, his voice uncharacteristically solemn and sobering. "They're expanding their territory and more."

Ace halts his restless pacing, hands clenching into fists. A line of sweat trickles down his spine—a familiar sensation whenever life throws him a curveball that has nothing to do with love or redemption, but everything to do with survival. Thoughts of Melanie flood his mind—her smile, her unwavering faith, the gentle cadence of her voice when she spoke of hope and grace.

'How could I bring her into this world, where threats lurk in every shadow?' He asked himself.

Jax crosses his arms, his brows furrowing with concern. "We knew they wouldn't back down easily. But we need specifics, Danny. What kind of expansion are we talking about?"

Danny's lips curl into a grim line. "Let's just say they're no longer sticking to drugs and guns," he replies, the gravity in his tone weighing heavily upon us.

Tre chuckles mirthlessly, his voice tinged with bitter sarcasm. "What's next? Are they going to sell Bibles and choir robes?"

"Tre," Ace warn, his voice a thunderous clap that silences his younger brother instantly. He turns back to Danny, his protective instincts for Melanie clashing with the remnants of a man who once believed he could outrun his past.

Jax, solid and stoic, leans against a metal column, crossing his arms over his chest. His eyes remain fixed on Danny, analyzing every word and gesture. Tre, always the wildcard, sits on the edge of a table, swinging a leg idly while his gaze remains sharp and focused.

Danny exhales slowly, drawing the shadows closer around him like a shroud. "The Moretti's are moving quicker than we anticipated," he says, laying out photos and documents as if unveiling statistical charts that predict an ominous future. "They're tightening their grip on the East Coast, and I've received word on their latest moves. It's worse than any of us thought."

Ace leaned forward, muscles tensing like steel cables beneath his skin. His amber eyes lock with Danny's, demanding answers in their unwavering gaze. The silence stretches, each second elongated into eternity until Danny finally speaks.

"They're deeply involved in human trafficking now," he confesses, his words landing like stones into the quiet pond of the dimly lit room. Ripples of horror spread outward, shattering the fragile peace that once graced the space. "They're been targeting the wives, girlfriends, and children of their enemies."

Shock courses through their veins like an electric surge, hitting them with the force of a physical blow. Ace's face, usually a mask of confidence and control, drains of color as the implications of Danny's words settle in.

"Jesus," Ace muttered under his breath, hands balling into fists as if ready to strike out against an unseen enemy. The reality of the threat loomed over him, like a dark cloud threatening to burst at any moment.

"Those bastards have no soul," Jax growls, his voice threading through the thick atmosphere like venomous tendrils matching the darkness that surrounds the men.

Danny nodded solemnly. "It's a whole new level of depravity, even for them."

"Melanie..." Ace can't stop her name from escaping his lips. His thoughts spin a discordant tune, every beat pulsating with concern for the woman who unknowingly wandered too close to the inferno of his world.

"Dammit!" He curses, slamming a clenched fist onto the table. The sound reverberates off the walls—a symphony of fury and fear. His brothers flinch at the sudden explosion of sound, but they understand all too well the source of his torment.

The dimly lit room seems to recoil from the weight of silence that follows Danny's revelation and Ace's eruption of frustration. He paces back and forth as a solitary figure by the window, staring into the darkness as if seeking an answer hidden within its depths. The silhouette of his broad shoulders is tense, his posture rigid against the backdrop of night.

"You're thinking about the wedding, aren't you?" Jax's voice cuts through the stillness like a blade poised between caution and urgency.

Ace turns to face him, movements deliberate yet filled with conflict. "She has nothing to do with this," He whispers, the muscle in his jaw pulsating with tension. "If we bring her into our mess, she becomes a target—a bargaining chip."

"Then we shield her," Danny suggests, his words hollow even to his own ears.

"Shield her?" Ace scoffs, pacing intensifying as the caged lion within prowls beneath the surface. Each step is a beat in the symphony of internal struggle—a crescendo of protective instinct clashing with love. "How do we shield someone from shadows that lurk behind every corner? From monsters disguised as men?"

"Have faith, brother," Tre interjects, though he avoids meeting Ace's gaze, understanding all too well the gravity of their dilemma.

"Faith." The word lingers on Ace's tongue, both bitter and sweet. "Faith is what I had when I walked away from her once, believing it was for the best. Faith brought us back together. And now... now faith asks me to choose between her safety and... and confronting the damn Moretti."

"Sometimes, faith demands sacrifice," Tre says, his voice steady as he steps forward.

Ace halts abruptly, chest heaving with suppressed emotion. "Not her," He whisper fiercely. "I've sacrificed enough. I won't let her pay the price for my past sins."

"What's your move, then?" Jax asks, watching him closely.

"I don't know," Ace confesses, the thought alone tightening a vice around his chest. "I just know that losing her again would shatter me beyond repair."

A low hum emanates from a distant generator, daring to punctuate the heavy silence in the dimly lit room. Shadows cling to the walls like silent conspirators, listening intently as the Andreas brothers face off over an issue that strikes too close to home.

"Look, Ace," Jax begins, his voice a calming force in the brewing storm. "I know what Melanie means to you, but you have to think straight here. The Moretti won't hesitate to use her against you, whether you're married or not. We need to ensure her safety first—before anything else."

My gaze flickers to Jax, noting his furrowed brow and set jaw. I sense the protective undertone that always underscores his words, especially when it comes to family.

"Jax is right," Ace murmurs, hands unconsciously balling into fists at the thought of Melanie caught in this ugly web. "She's... she's everything." His voice trails off, revealing the chink in his armor.

"Everything, huh?" Tre interjects with a smirk, though his eyes convey a seriousness that matched Ace's. "Then how can we sit back and let these goons continue their reign of terror? Our best shot at taking them down is now when we still have the element of surprise on our side."

"Surprise doesn't outweigh safety, Tre," Jax counters, his stance firm like an unyielding oak. "We're talking about human lives here—Melanie's life."

"Human lives are exactly why we can't back down!" Tre's hands gesture emphatically, mirroring the passion in his voice. "If we don't stop them, more innocent people will suffer. This isn't just about Melanie; it's about doing what's right."

"Doing what's right," Ace echoes softly, his thoughts a discordant melody as he tries to harmonize his love for Melanie with the duty to protect her and others from harm. He envisions their wedding aisle, once a path to joy, now potentially lined with threats and shadows.

"Man, I get it. But if we play this wrong, there might not be a 'happily ever after' for anyone," Jax argues, his deep voice resonating with the weight of his conviction.

"Since when did we start playing it wrong, Jax?" Tre challenges, a wild note in his tone that speaks of his willingness to risk it all. "We've never backed down from a fight before. Why start now?"

"Because now, Tre," Ace cut in sharply, voice returning like the crescendo of a battle hymn, "now we have something—or someone—to lose that matters more than winning."

"Isn't that all the more reason to fight harder?" Tre counters, leaning forward as if his physical proximity could sway his brother's resolve.

"Harder, yes. Recklessly, no," Jax says, moving to stand shoulder to shoulder with Ace. "We need a plan that keeps Melanie out of their crosshairs."

"Plans are good," Tre concedes reluctantly, the fire dimming in his eyes. "But let's not forget who we're dealing with. The Moretti's won't stop until they're stopped."

I nod slowly, my mind racing through a thousand different scenarios, each with its own inherent risks. The melody of Melanie's laughter rings in my ears—a bittersweet reminder of what's at stake. "Then we'll find a way—a way to keep her safe and put an end to this. But Melanie comes first."

"Agreed," Jax says, relief softening his features.

"Fine," Tre sighs, throwing up his hands in exasperation. "But let's be clear: this isn't us running scared. It's us fighting strategically."

"Strategically," Ace repeat, the word resonating in the hollow room like a solemn vow. And in that moment, a decision crystallizes within him—sharp and as unavoidable as the final note in a requiem. "I think I may need to rejoin the ranks."

"Going back to the Basito's, Ace... it's not just stepping back into the ring; it's inviting the devil to dance," Jax murmurs, his voice barely above a whisper, as if afraid to disturb the fragile peace that has descended upon us.

"I know. But if it keeps her safe, I'll do whatever needs to be done." His grip tightened, fingers pressing into his palms until the skin paled.

Memories of Melanie's infectious smile and the gentle touch of her hand lingered in his mind, precious treasures he vowed to safeguard at any cost. The idea of returning to the Basito's sent a shiver down his spine, like swallowing shards of glass that tore at his insides, clashing with the newfound convictions he held so dear.

"Melanie wouldn't stand for this. She sees the real you," Tre remarked, searching Ace's face for a glimpse of the brother buried beneath his tough exterior.

"Love sometimes demands unthinkable choices," Ace countered, pain flickering in his honey-colored eyes. "She may resent me for it, but she'll be alive to feel that way."

The dim light of the single bulb overhead flickered, casting eerie shadows across the four men as a heavy silence settled in the room. Ace's jaw clenched, his hands rested flat against the table, the veins in his forearms standing out like cords.

"Plus.... It doesn't matter anyway. As of now the wedding-our engagement—it's off." Ace bit out, his voice low and unwavering.

His brothers' eyes snapped to his, and a collective gasp sucked the remaining air from the claustrophobic space. Danny's mouth opened, but no words came out as he processed the gravity of Ace's declaration.

"Off?" Jax's tone was incredulous, his brows knitting together in confusion.

"Are you—" Tre started, but Ace raised a hand to silence him.

"Melanie's safety comes before everything," Ace stated, his honey-colored eyes reflecting the unyielding resolve that steeled his frame. "I won't let her become another victim to the Moretti' vendettas."

"Damn right," Danny finally found his voice, nodding in agreement. "You're making the hard choice, brother, but it's the right one."

"Hard doesn't begin to cover it," Ace muttered under his breath, his heart constricting at the thought of Melanie's face when he would break the news. His mind's eye painted her expressive brown eyes clouded with confusion and hurt.

"Then what's the plan?" Jax asked, leaning forward, his elbows pressing into the scarred wood of the table. He looked every bit the warrior they were bred to be, ready to follow his brother into the depths of hell if needed.

Ace's gaze remained steady, though his spirit was a tempest. "We tighten our defenses—we watch everyone connected to us like hawks—"

"An' we hit back," Tre interjected, his fists clenched on the tabletop. "We can't let them think they've got us on the ropes."

"No," Ace corrected, a silent symphony of melancholy echoing through his soul. "We disappear from their radar. We make them believe they've won until we can dismantle their operations from the inside."

"Disappear," Jax repeated, skepticism lacing his tone. "And leave Melanie?"

"Temporarily," Ace assured, though the very suggestion tore at him more than any physical wound could. "It's the only way I can keep her out of the crossfire."

The room fell silent again, the tension palpable, as they all considered the implications of such drastic measures.

"An' what about after?" Tre's voice was barely above a whisper, the question hanging between them like a fragile note threatening to shatter.

"God willing, there'll be an 'after'," Ace replied, a fervent prayer accompanying his words.

Tre shook his head, frustration etching lines into his brow. "And what about your soul, Ace? You walk that path again—you might not come back."

"The day I let Melanie down is the day I lose my soul anyway," Ace said, the finality in his voice leaving no room for argument.

With each heartbeat, Ace felt the gravity of his choice anchoring him to a reality he wished he could escape. The echoes of hymns from long-ago Sundays filled the space around him, reminding him of the innocence he once shared with Melanie—a time before bloodstains and betrayal.

"Then we stand with you," Jax declared, placing a firm hand on Ace's shoulder.

Danny whispered, "Whatever it takes."

"Whatever it takes," Tre echoed reluctantly, understanding the necessity of sacrifice.

"Then let's prepare for war," Ace agreed, feeling the weight of command settle upon him yet again. He straightened, his imposing figure casting a long shadow across the room as if to challenge the very darkness itself. The melody of Melanie's favorite song whispered through his mind, a sweet yet sorrowful refrain, promising redemption amidst the chaos.

"Let's pray we're making the right call," Tre sighed, the words themselves a prayer.

"Right or wrong, we're doing it together," Ace stated, his eyes narrowing, the decision etched into every line of his body.

As the men huddled closer, an unspoken oath hung in the air, binding them to a course that could redeem or ruin them all. But for Ace, the path was clear—every step forward was a step toward protecting the woman who held his heart, the woman whose love composed the very symphony of his existence.

"Alright then, let's get movin'. Time is something we don't have the luxury of wasting," Jax said, standing up and signaling the end of their council of war.

"Hey," Ace called out as they began to disperse, pausing them mid-step. "Keep this between us. Not a word to Melanie, not yet."

"Understood," they chorused, solemn as altar boys.

In the dim light, shadows danced around them as a heavy silence settled over the room. Ace's jaw clenched as he leaned against the table, veins bulging on his forearms.

As the others departed one by one, Ace lingered behind in the shadows of past choices and looming consequences—carrying the weight of leadership like heavy chains upon tired shoulders. Ace fumbled in his pockets, retrieving the small azure box intended for Melanie. Gently lifting the lid, he gazed at the cross and locket nestled inside. The cross was his mother's, and the locket was custom designed to match, containing two pictures capturing their journey. One snapshot from their high school days a decade ago, and another portraying their rekindled love.

The image of Melanie gliding down the aisle adorned with his ring and necklace filled his mind, evoking a mix of emotions that threatened to spill over in tears. Taking a deep breath to compose himself, he prepared for the pivotal conversation ahead.

"Grant me strength," Ace murmured softly into the emptiness around him, his heart's silent melody harmonizing with the shadows enveloping him. Though redemption seemed like a distant dream, he clung to it as tightly as he held onto the love propelling his sacrifices. As tranquility settled in, Ace steeled himself for the uncertain horizon awaiting with each passing moment.

TWENTY

The Light of Hope

The sun dipped low, bathing Ace's opulent living room in a golden hue. She sat cross-legged on the plush carpet, her wedding planner sprawled open like a treasure map in her lap. Her fingers, adorned with soft blush nail polish matching her wedding theme, danced over venue sketches and seating arrangements, each stroke a brushstroke in the masterpiece of her upcoming nuptials.

Ace trudged through the door and slumped into the armchair opposite her, his voice gravelly as he began, "Hey Mel, we need to talk." His tattoos seemed to shift restlessly on his arms and neck, mirroring the tension in his posture.

Looking up, Melanie's expressive brown eyes met Ace's distraught gaze. The seriousness etched on his face set her heart pounding an anxious beat.

"What's going on?" she asked, sensing the gravity of the moment.

Ace leaned forward, elbows resting on his knees as he struggled to find the right words. "We finally met up with Danny last night." he started hesitantly. "He's got some troubling info about the Moretti family... it's bad news."

A chill ran down Melanie's spine at Ace's revelation. "What kind of information?" she inquired, her voice barely above a whisper.

"They've been targeting women from rival families for... for unspeakable things," Ace explained grimly. The unspoken dread hung heavy between them.

Her wedding plans forgotten; Melanie felt her world tilt off its axis. "Oh God..." Her hand flew to her mouth in shock.

Ace stood up abruptly and began pacing the room as if wrestling with an invisible foe. "I can't risk your safety," he declared firmly. "We have to put off the wedding indefinitely."

"Delay?" The word tasted bitter on Melanie's tongue. "Ace, we can't let fear control us or dictate our future together," she argued passionately.

His frustration mounting, Ace raised his voice in desperation. "Mel, this is about keeping you safe! I can't bear the thought of something happening to you."

Standing up to face him head-on, Melanie grounded herself in her faith and resolve. "I appreciate your concern, but fear isn't our guide here and you're not walking away from me again," she asserted gently but firmly.

Their eyes locked in a silent exchange of emotions; understanding passed between them like an unspoken vow.

"Help me find another way," Ace implored as he reached out to intertwine their hands.

"Always," Melanie replied with unwavering determination. Their unity, a beacon amidst the uncertainty and danger that lay ahead.

The Andreas family living room exuded a sense of urgency, a departure from its usual somber ambiance with dark wood furniture and heavy drapes. Ace paced restlessly as Melanie sat on the edge of her seat, hands tightly clasped in her lap, trying to hold together their fragile situation.

"Hey everyone, this is Samantha Thompson," Ace introduced, nodding towards the confident woman who had just entered from the guest room.

"Actually, it's just Sam," she smoothly corrected with a quick nod. Tre smirked knowingly, but no one pressed for details.

"Melanie has a plan," Ace announced, his voice steady despite the turmoil inside him—a mix of fear and determination buoyed by Melanie's unwavering faith. "Let's hear it," Jax encouraged, his protective gaze fixed on Melanie.

"So here's the deal," Melanie began, cutting through the tension. "Ace's history with the Basito's could work in our favor. They want that casino deal closed—what if we leverage that against the Moretti?"

"Go on," Thomas prompted, a hint of softness in his stern expression at the prospect of keeping his son out of their criminal world.

"We suggest a partnership," Melanie explained, her eyes sparkling with strategic insight. "We invite the entire Moretti clan to our wedding as a gesture of goodwill."

"Playing nice with enemies?" Tre pondered with interest.

"Exactly," Melanie affirmed confidently.

"It's about uniting against a common threat." Thomas nodded thoughtfully, acknowledging the plan's potential to safeguard Ace's newfound love.

"Keep planning as if nothing's wrong; they'll think Ace isn't onto them." Danny chimed in, "I can set up a meeting with Rocco Moretti to make it look legit and start negotiations."

Though tasting bitter like ash in his mouth, Ace recognized an odd harmony amidst chaos—a opus of deception they had to orchestrate flawlessly.

Ace met her gaze filled with love tinged by fear and strength anchored by faith—an internal struggle he faced daily between shadows and light.

"Alright," Ace declared decisively amidst the flurry of activity that ensued after their agreement to proceed with the wedding plan dipped in strategy—a future composed step by step on faith's wings.

The atmosphere in Ace's home office crackled with tension, like a simmering pot waiting for the right ingredients. Blueprints of the casino sprawled over the mahogany desk, while photos Melanie and his family adorned the walls, and multiple laptop screens cast a glow on intent faces.

Jax spoke up, his voice calm and low as he gestured at various entry points on the blueprints. "Surveillance is our best bet. We need eyes everywhere."

Danny nodded, fingers tapping away at his keyboard. "I can set up hidden cameras for live feeds."

Sam leaned in with a furrowed brow. "We also need an insider they won't suspect."

Tre's playful smirk turned to Melanie. "What about our gospel artist here? You've got a way with words, Mel. Maybe you can charm those goons into revealing their secrets."

Melanie blushed but met Tre's gaze head-on. “If it helps, count me in. My voice isn't just for singing hymns.”

Thomas chimed in with newfound respect in his tone. "Melanie is right. Courage and faith can conquer even the toughest challenges."

Ace observed silently, feeling each mention of danger involving Melanie like a discordant note in his heart. She was his anchor, yet here they were, planning a risky move that could shatter everything.

Finally taking charge, Ace assigned roles. "Danny, tech is your domain—surveillance and bugs."

Jax and Tre were tasked as shadows to gather intel discreetly while Thomas would leverage his connections for information on the Moretti.

Sam was designated as Melanie's protector while Melanie herself vowed to be an unexpected presence among their enemies.

As Ace drew closer to Melanie, he couldn't help but express his concerns quietly. "Melanie, we're stepping into dangerous territory—are you sure about this?"

Her response was unwavering. "David didn't need armor against Goliath—just faith."

Ace's resolve solidified at her words. "I'll add prayer and strategy to my arsenal," he agreed.

After discussing plans regarding the Basito family and Vincent Basito specifically, Sam redirected their focus back to their mission.

With each member leaving the meeting room carrying their part of the plan—a verse to remember or a role to play—Ace found himself silently praying for guidance through the storm ahead.

For love and a brighter future beyond their shadows, they would brave this storm together under God's guiding hand.

Twenty-One

A Tapestry of Trials

The room buzzed with determination as Ace scanned the group, each face a portrait of purpose. When Melanie's eyes met his, a silent understanding passed between them, a harmony of strength and resolve resonating in their gazes.

"Let's break it down," Ace declared, his voice commanding attention like a conductor leading an orchestra. "We've got two main fronts: the wedding and the operation."

"Wedding first," Melanie interjected firmly, her organizational skills shining through like a steadfast soprano amidst chaos. "It's happening in four weeks. Time's ticking."

"Four weeks," Tre mused, rubbing his stubbled chin in contemplation. "Tight but doable."

"We kick off surveillance in forty-eight hours," Jax updated, fingers dancing over his laptop keys like a skilled pianist. "Intel gathering starts then."

"Our undercover team needs at least two weeks to get in and gain trust," Sam added coolly, her voice steady and composed.

Ace nodded, mentally coordinating their next moves. "We proceed with wedding arrangements as planned to keep up appearances. Danny, you're on deck."

Danny whipped out his phone, its screen now a gateway to either salvation or ruin. "I'm on it." He dialed Rocco's office, the connection sounding like a bass drum thudding through Ace's chest. "It's Danny, I need to set up a meeting with Moretti about the casino deal."

"Good day, Mr. Carter. I'll see about Mr. Moretti's availability for a discussion soon," came the crisp response from the other end, unknowingly becoming part of their intricate scheme.

"Make it quick," Danny urged urgently. "Time is crucial."

"Understood," confirmed the voice before hanging up.

Ace clenched his fists discreetly as he watched Danny, tension building subtly. The plan was set in motion; the stakes had never been higher. In the ensuing silence, he could hear his own heartbeat alongside Melanie's unwavering faith grounding him.

"God is with us," Melanie whispered softly as she squeezed his hand reassuringly. "We're in this together."

Her touch was a calming melody amidst chaos—a reminder of love's transformative strength within him. Ace battled conflicting impulses: protect her or distance her from danger.

"We are," he affirmed finally as fear ebbed away, replaced by a resolute sense of purpose. "But I can't help but worry for you."

"Fear dissipates where love abides," she responded with conviction that cut through his uncertainties.

A faint smile graced Ace's lips as he pondered if their pursuit of harmony could ever match Melanie's unwavering faith purity-wise.

"Alright everyone," he addressed them all with determination. "Our roles are set; let's move forward prayerfully and precisely."

"Step by step," Thomas' resonant voice added gravitas. "We adapt as we go."

"Stay vigilant," Ace instructed firmly. "Safety first."

“Let’s make some magic,” Jax quipped lightly though seriousness lingered behind his gaze reflecting their mission’s gravity.

“Blessings,” Melanie corrected gently—her faith underlining their united resolve.

As they dispersed from the meeting room, Ace felt love and duty pulsing within him. With Melanie beside him and God guiding them, a future free from shadows seemed within reach.

The sun filtered through the blinds, painting stripes across Ace's study like a makeshift prison. Seated at his desk, he tapped his fingers nervously on the mahogany surface, each beat echoing the thud of his racing heart. Mentally preparing himself, he whispered, "Vincent Basito," before dialing the number.

"Vincent? It's Ace Andreas," he spoke firmly into the phone, concealing the tension coiled within him. A pregnant pause followed as Vincent processed the unexpected call.

"Ace," came Vincent's gruff response, tinged with surprise. "What's this about?"

"I need to discuss the casino deal in person. Can you meet me at the marina?" Ace's grip on the phone tightened, urgency lacing his words.

After a moment of deliberation, Vincent agreed to the meeting. As Ace hung up, relief mingled with apprehension. This conversation held immense weight; it could alter everything. Offering a silent prayer for guidance, he finished his coffee and slipped out of the house without disturbing Melanie.

Driving towards the marina, thoughts whirled in Ace's mind. The gravity of their situation loomed large - safety, future, purpose all hanging in the balance. Yet amidst uncertainty, faith anchored him. Pulling up at the deserted marina, spotting Vincent's car in the distance, Ace steeled himself for what lay ahead.

With resolve bolstered by belief that God walked beside him, Ace advanced towards what would be a pivotal moment—a testament to unwavering faith and divine intervention.

Twenty-Two

The Harmony of Healing

The first tendrils of dawn were unfurling like a gentle caress across the tranquil waters of the harbor, as the radiant beams of the morning sun caressed the polished chrome of an approaching black sedan. Its tinted windows were as impenetrable and mysterious as the waters below, mirroring the enigmatic presence of its occupant. Ace's grip tightened upon the cold metal railing, his heart thrumming against his ribcage in anticipation of a reunion tinged with apprehension.

"The Lord is my light and my salvation; whom shall I fear?" Ace murmured, drawing strength from his unwavering faith as he watched the car glide smoothly to a halt. The door swung open with practiced elegance, revealing Vincent Basito, a man whose very essence whispered of power and authority, garbed in an impeccably tailored suit that accentuated his muscular physique. His silent retinue emerged from behind him, their dark eyes observant and unwavering, like sentinels attentive to the whims of their master.

The early morning silence was shattered by Ace's baritone call, "Vince!" The voice that reverberated through the air carried the weight of years spent forging alliances and battling adversity. The two men exchanged a nod of mutual respect before Ace descended the steps to meet Vincent on equal footing.

"Ah, Ace." Vincent greeted him with a firm handshake that conveyed a semblance of camaraderie beneath its veneer of command. "You're early." Vincent regarded Ace with a gaze that spoke volumes - one that had navigated countless storms in pursuit of dominion over turbulent seas.

Ace replied evenly, unperturbed by his companion's scrutiny, "Didn't want to keep you waiting." His measured footsteps echoed rhythmically against the pavement as he approached Vincent's group. His countenance only betrayed a fraction of the turmoil rioting within; this encounter held paramount significance for him, and his demeanor radiated resolute determination.

Vincent bestowed upon him a slight nod – not as an acknowledgment but rather an invitation to proceed. Flanked by his formidable guards, their silent vigilance exuded an unmistakable air of influence and primacy. With measured grace, they fell into step behind their leader as if orchestrating an unspoken symphony that thrummed in harmony with their surroundings.

"Let's cut to the chase, Ace," Vincent urged without preamble, his tone embodying both firmness and authority. "What do you need from me?"

The question settled heavily upon Ace like a yoke forged from lead; however, he bore it with stoic dignity befitting a man who had faced insurmountable trials head-on.

"I understand the stakes," Ace replied steadfastly, meeting Vincent's penetrating gaze without flinching. "And I'm not here to waste your time."

As if sensing Ace's trepidation, Vincent paused mid-step, turning to face him directly. His piercing gaze seemed to strip away layers until only raw honesty remained between them.

"Before we get to that," Vincent clarified pointedly, "know this – I don't take kindly to betrayal or wasted time. You've got one shot at convincing me why I should risk my neck for your cause."

A profound hush fell over them as they stood locked in silence- two warriors bound by common goals yet separated by divergent paths they had each chosen to traverse. In that momentary stillness echoed the words of Proverbs 27:17: "As iron sharpens iron, so one person sharpens another." It was then that Ace drew upon his deepest reservoirs of courage and conviction:

"I am here because the Moretti's are threatening everything we've all worked so hard for and everything I stand for," Ace confessed earnestly, each word resonating with quiet fervor. "Your experience, your connections... they can make all the difference." He paused briefly before continuing: "I wouldn't ask if it wasn't important."

Vincent inclined his head slightly in acquiescence before resuming their march towards destiny. His expression softened perceptibly as he queried further: "Important enough to put my family on the line?"

At this juncture, Ace could not help but acknowledge the profound impact such an alliance would entail - more than just mafia ties or strategic partnerships.

"Your family," Ace emphasized gravely, imbuing every syllable with solemn reverence. "This is about protecting your family. It's about securing a future where our families aren't haunted by shadows." He took a deep breath before proceeding with unwavering resolve: "I may no longer be a part of your family, but we're still connected - I have faith that you'll see my side of things."

Vincent responded thoughtfully after considering Ace's impassioned plea: "Faith is a luxury in our world," he agreed contemplatively. "But I sense your faith runs deeper than mere lip service." He studied Ace shrewdly before continuing: "Belief can be a potent ally or formidable adversary."

Acknowledging their shared understanding regarding matters of faith and loyalty, Ace nodded solemnly: "Indeed."

"Show why your faith is so strong, that I'll help you out on this Ace." Vincent folded his arms over his chest, daring Ace to convince him.

The marina was still as Ace unrolled the blueprint of his scheme, the water around them a mirror reflecting back the gravity of their clandestine meeting. His finger traced the lines and intersections as if they were notes on a score, each one leading to a crescendo that could topple the Moretti' empire.

"Here," Ace said, tapping a particular spot on the paper spread between them. "This is where they move their product, under the guise of legitimate business. It's all there—dates, transactions, the lot." His voice held an edge, like a violin string pulled taut with urgency.

Vincent leaned forward, the moonlight glinting off his eyes, turning them into pools of dark scrutiny. He had the look of a man who'd seen every trick in the book, yet here he was, poring over Ace's plan with the focus of a maestro dissecting a new symphony.

"Your sources are solid?" Vincent's question was not one of doubt but of due diligence, the careful probing of a strategist.

"Solid and ready to testify," Ace affirmed. He watched the older man's face, searching for any sign of hesitation or retreat. But Vincent's expression was unreadable—a mask carved from years of navigating treacherous waters.

Ace felt the tension in his shoulders, a physical manifestation of the silent battle waging within him. Here he was, laying bare the vulnerabilities of those he cared for, offering up a confession to this man who could either absolve or condemn him.

"Point out the weak spots," Vincent commanded, his attention never wavering from the intricate web of information laid before him.

"Here, and here." Ace's fingers hovered over key locations, the hubs of activity that kept the Moretti machine oiled and operational. "They think they're untouchable, but we can prove otherwise."

Vincent nodded slowly, absorbing every detail with the precision of a composer learning the subtleties of a new piece. The docks, so often filled with the cacophony of daily commerce, were hushed now, as though waiting for the downbeat of an unseen conductor's baton.

The night air carried the scent of salt and diesel—a harsh reminder of the world they occupied, where the sweet fragrance of redemption seemed forever out of reach. Yet, in this moment, Ace clung to the belief that even the most discordant chords could be resolved, that faith could harmonize with action, and together they could craft a melody of justice.

"Timing will be everything," Vincent finally said, his voice a low thrum that matched the rhythm of the lapping waves. "We strike when they least expect it, throw them off their game."

Ace exhaled slowly, letting go of the breath he hadn't realized he'd been holding. There was a kinship in their shared focus, a recognition that while they may have danced to different tunes in the past, now they moved in time to the same beat—a dance of retribution and hope intertwined.

"Your family will be shielded," Vincent added, sealing the promise with the gravity of his gaze. "I take no pleasure in the suffering of innocents."

"Thank you," Ace murmured, feeling the weight of the words. They were more than a mere expression of gratitude; they were an acknowledgment of the price of this alliance, the cost of stepping into the light when shadows beckoned with seductive whispers.

"Let's finalize the steps," Vincent said, rolling up the blueprint as if closing a sacred text.

Ace nodded, his heart pounding a steady tattoo in his chest. This was it—the beginning of the end of his old life. Ace shifted his weight, the gravel beneath his boots crunching an uneven rhythm as he faced Vincent. The marina, with its bobbing boats and creaking docks, seemed to pause for a moment—as if the sea itself held its breath, attuned to the gravity of their clandestine meeting.

"Vincent," Ace began, his voice steady despite the tempest raging within him. "I know we've got a plan to take down the Moretti, but we can't ignore the darkness they're feeding into." He locked eyes with Vincent, the honey hues of his irises smoldering with a fervent intensity. "The sex trafficking ring they're running—it's not just a threat to our families. It's a scourge on entire communities."

Vincent's face remained impassive, but his clenched jaw betrayed his inner turmoil. "I've heard the whispers, Ace," he said quietly. "Every corner of the Metro seems to echo with them—tales of young lives stolen; futures silenced before they even begin. It sickens me."

"Then you understand why we need to act fast," Ace pressed, his tattoos shifting with the flex of his muscles, as if the inked stories etched into his skin were clamoring for justice.

"Of course I do," Vincent replied, the frustration in his voice rising like a discordant note. "But the whispers are just that—whispers. We've been grasping at shadows, chasing phantoms without form. Until now, we've had no solid leads."

"Which is why we need to amplify our efforts," Ace countered, the desperation threading through his words. "We have the chance to cut through the noise, to bring light into this darkness."

Vincent's gaze shifted out to the horizon where the sun was beginning to sink, setting the sky ablaze with streaks of crimson and gold. A silent prayer seemed to pass through him, a plea for guidance amidst the storm of temptation and sin.

"Faith alone won't dismantle this evil, Vincent. We need action." Ace's tone softened, carrying the melody of a man who knew too well the siren's call of a troubled past, yet yearned for redemption.

"Action needs direction, Ace," Vincent retorted, turning back to meet Ace's earnest stare. "And your intel could be the compass we've been searching for."

"Then let's navigate these treacherous waters together," Ace suggested, the determination in his voice resonating with the unwavering beat of a drum. "Let's end their perverse symphony once and for all."

Vincent nodded slowly, the decision etching itself into the lines of his face. "Agreed. But we'll need to orchestrate our moves precisely. Any misstep could put more lives at risk."

"Understood," Ace acknowledged, the promise reflected in his stance, strong and unyielding. The two men stood in silence, both aware of the cacophony of challenges ahead, yet united by a shared resolve to restore harmony to a world off-key.

"Let's get to work," Vincent finally said, his voice carrying the command of a maestro ready to lead his ensemble to victory.

Ace felt the chord of hope resonate within him. Together, they would compose a new narrative—one where love triumphed over hatred, and faith overcame fear. The first step in their concerto of redemption had been taken, and there was no turning back.

Twenty-Three

Whispers of Wisdom

Four Weeks Later

The crackle of the fireplace sang a hymn to the twilight hour, its golden light casting long shadows across the living room where two silhouettes moved in harmony. Melanie's fingers traced the spines of books on the shelf as she waited for Ace to return with the last of their luggage. She had been staying in his guest room, a space that now held the whispers of her laughter and the scent of her lavender perfume.

"Almost ready," Ace said, returning with a leather duffle bag that seemed out of place amid the softness of Melanie's luggage. He dropped the bag and reached for her, pulling her into an unexpected dance, their bodies swaying gently before the flickering flames.

"Will you miss me?" he asked, his voice a low rumble that resonated with the fire's bass. His honey-colored eyes searched hers, seeking reassurance even as concern laced his tone. "You'll be here Sam, but you won't be alone – security will always be around, but out of sight."

Melanie's lips curved into a smile, the warmth from the hearth mirrored in her gaze. "Definitely not lonely," she assured him, her voice steady like the metronome that guided her choir. "But I will miss you. Sam knows how to make me laugh, though. We'll be fine."

Ace pulled Melanie close and pulled out a velvet box from his pocket, holding it out with a hint of a smile.

"I have something for you," he said, his deep voice laced with warmth. "My wedding gift to you."

Melanie's eyes widened as she took the box, her fingers trembling slightly. She lifted the lid to reveal a delicate gold chain holding a beautiful filigree diamond cross and a diamond encrusted locket nestled inside.

"The cross was my mother's," Ace continued. "She wanted me to give it to..." He paused, holding Melanie's gaze. "...someone special."

Melanie's breath caught in her throat. She recognized the significance of this gift, a family heirloom from his beloved mother. They matched her engagement ring perfectly.

Opening the locket, on the left was the last picture they had taken together in high school just days before he disappeared and on the right was the night Ace asked her to marry him.

"Ace, I don't know what to say," she whispered as tears surfaced. "It's beautiful. Thank you."

He gently lifted the necklace from the box and moved behind her to clasp it around her neck. His fingers grazed her skin, sending a shiver down her spine. The cross and locket came to rest just above her heart.

Melanie touched the necklace reverently, overcome with emotion. This was more than just a gift - it was a symbol of Ace's trust and affection. Proof of the future he saw with her.

Her eyes met his, a silent understanding passing between them. With this necklace, Ace was entrusting Melanie with his heart.

Melanie's fingers traced the delicate contours of the cross, lost in thought. This necklace represented so much more than she could put into words.

It was a piece of Ace's past, an heirloom imbued with his mother's love. The woman who had shaped him into the man he was today. The locket was proof that Ace was a man willing to change, to leave his old life behind for the promise of a new beginning with her. Wearing this meant accepting the man beneath the tough exterior. It meant believing in his capacity for redemption, no matter his past sins.

Melanie clasped the necklace tightly, feeling its edges dig into her palm. This was confirmation that life with Ace was a leap of faith she was willing to take. With Ace by her side, she finally believed they could build something beautiful from the ashes of their past.

Melanie took a deep breath and met Ace's gaze. "I don't even know how to thank you for such a meaningful gift. This...this means the world to me."

Ace nodded, his eyes never leaving hers.

"It's beautiful," Melanie said softly. She gently removed the necklace from the box and held it in her open palm. The diamonds glimmered under the lights. "I can feel how much love and history is contained in these. I'll treasure it always."

"I'm glad you like it," Ace said gruffly. "I know that my mother would have wanted you to have her cross. She was a strong believer, just like you."

Melanie's voice trembled with raw emotion as she cut him off, her heart pounding in her chest. "God had a plan all along," she whispered. "He brought you back into my life for a reason. I was lost, still clinging to imaginary fairy tale princes and knight. But now it all makes sense."

Her warm brown eyes blazed with determination and love as she continued, "I didn't need a knight in shining armor. I need a warrior clad in the full armor of God. And you, Ace, are that man."

Ace leaned down, pressing his forehead to hers, allowing her love and warmth to seep into him, fortifying his resolve, as his heart thrummed in his chest.

Grabbing her hand, he pulled her into a slow dance. Melanie laid her head on Ace's chest and beathed in his scent as he led her around the living room in a rare moment of peace and serenity. Their moment was interrupted by the sharp ring of the phone, an unwelcome intruder in their moment of communion.

Ace tensed, the subtle shift in his muscles betraying his composure as he released Melanie to answer the call. Upon seeing the caller ID, his heart hammered against his ribcage, echoing the ringing that refused to be ignored.

Ace cupped Melanie's face, "why don't you make sure Sam has everything she needs for the night, and I'll come and get you before I leave?"

Melanie understood; a silent sentinel aware of the battle within him. Her own heart fluttered with apprehension, sensing the gravity of the call, her trust in him unwavering.

She turned her face to kiss his palm and went to check on Sam giving Ace the privacy he desired.

The music of their earlier dance fading into a distant memory, replaced by the dissonant chords of uncertainty. She prayed silently, her faith a shield against the darkness that threatened to encroach upon their sanctuary.

Twenty-Four

Threads of Trust

He crossed the room with purposeful strides, every step measured and heavy as he ran thick tatted fingers through his sandy brown hair. "Hello?" The word escaped his lips, guarded yet resolute, a warrior answering the challenge at his gate.

"Rocco Moretti," came the voice on the other end, a name that carried weight, a history that bled into the present.

At the sound of Rocco's voice, Ace's grip on the phone tightened, knuckles whitening as he fought to maintain his facade.

"Ah, Rocco," Ace managed, his voice strained through the veneer of politeness. "To what do I owe the pleasure?"

"Congratulations on the wedding, Ace," Rocco Moretti's voice slithered through the phone line like a serpent winding its way through Eden. His tone was menacing, wrapped in a deceptive smile that could be heard but not seen. "Can't wait to meet your beautiful bride tomorrow."

Ace felt as if a cold hand had reached into his chest and squeezed. He pressed the phone harder against his ear, his other hand clenching into a fist at his side. "Thanks, Rocco. We're looking forward to it," he lied with practiced ease, his voice steady despite the tremor of dread that threatened to betray him.

"And then there's the little matter of our deal—the casino sale." Rocco's voice dropped an octave, heavy with implication. "I trust everything will go smoothly?"

"Of course," Ace replied, the words bitter on his tongue. "Just a formality at this point."

"Good. Because you know how I hate... surprises." The threat in Rocco's voice was unmistakable, a dark undercurrent beneath the cordial surface.

Ace ended the call with a curt farewell, feeling as though he'd just navigated a minefield. He stood motionless for a moment, the silence of the room amplifying the roar of blood in his ears.

He remembered their slow dance earlier; the way Melanie had looked up at him with such trust and adoration. How could he protect her from men like Rocco Moretti—men who saw life as nothing more than a game of power and dominance?

As the fire crackled and popped, Ace imagined a different kind of music—the haunting melody of a future where Melanie's laughter was silenced by fear. He couldn't let that happen. He wouldn't. Whatever it took, he would shield her from the tempest that was Rocco Moretti, even if it meant standing alone against the storm.

Steeling himself, Ace turned to face whatever came next, armed with the knowledge that his love for Melanie was his greatest weapon. It was a love forged in adversity, tempered by faith, and it would not break easily.

Ace's hand hovered over the phone, as if distancing himself from Rocco Moretti's venomous words could somehow shield him from their impact. The device, once innocuous and silent on the mahogany coffee table, now felt like an instrument of malice. He let out a ragged breath, his fingers trembling against the warm wood.

"Lord, give me strength," he whispered under his breath, a prayer that was more habit than conviction at this moment.

The room seemed to close in around him, each tick of the grandfather clock a reminder of the relentless march towards a future suddenly smeared with uncertainty. His eyes swept over the packed suitcases by the door—symbols of a honeymoon that promised joy yet now whispered danger.

The crackle of the fire played a discordant melody to his spiraling thoughts. Ace had always been one to take risks, but when those risks threatened Melanie's well-sculpted life, the stakes became terrifyingly real. She was as meticulous with her dreams as she was with her music—every note had to be perfect, every harmony just so. And here he was, introducing a cacophony into her carefully arranged symphony.

"Rocco thinks he's got the upper hand," Ace said aloud, his voice steadier now, laced with determination.

He stood, the resolve hardening in his gaze as he looked at his reflection in the windowpane—the ghostly image of a soul entwined in battle against an unseen enemy. The music of their lives had changed, the rhythm disrupted, but Ace wouldn't let the dance end—not on Rocco Moretti's terms.

"Melanie believes in redemption... in second chances," Ace reminded himself, the ember of courage within him fanned by the memory of her steadfast faith. "I won't let her down."

With each step he took towards the mantle, his resolve grew stronger. He picked up a framed photograph of him and Melanie, a captured moment of laughter and light. It was that laughter he would fight for, that light he would defend.

TWENTY-FIVE

The Melody of Miracles

Sunlight streamed through the fabric covered gazebo, casting a kaleidoscope of colors across Melanie and Ace as they stood before the altar. The grandeur of their outdoor wedding paled in comparison to the intense emotion that filled the air, reflected in the big, expressive brown eyes of Melanie. She gazed up at Ace, the former breaker of her heart to now soon-to-be husband, his tall frame and honey-colored eyes exuding an aura of protective strength.

"Melanie," Ace began, his eyes locked onto hers, trembling slightly as he spoke his vows. "I promise to cherish and protect you, to guide and support you in our walk with God. I know I've made mistakes in my past, but my love for you is my redemption. I stand before God, our families, and friends, to take you as my wife. Not just in this life, but for all eternity."

Her heart swelled with love and faith as she listened to his vows, words she never imagined he'd say, especially not after their tumultuous past. But here they were, surrendering to a future neither expected but both desired deeply.

"Ace," Melanie replied, her voice filled with emotion and conviction, "I take you with all your scars and battles, as my husband. Together, we will create a symphony of forgiveness and grace, harmonizing through faith and love. I vow to stand by your side, to help you grow in your faith, and to be your rock when life gets hard. I will trust in God to lead us through this journey as one."

They exchanged rings, sealing their commitment to each other and their eyes met, as something shifted between them. In that moment, their past pains melted away, leaving only the promise of a new beginning. Melanie's brown eyes, softened as she looked up at Ace. His gaze, once so cold, now ignited with an ember of something that made her heart trip.

"Ladies and gentlemen," Pastor Harris boomed proudly, startling them from their trance, "presenting for the first time, Mr. and Mrs. Ace and Melanie Andreas!"

As the pastor pronounced them man and wife, and Ace kissed her with a tenderness that belied his tough exterior, there was a collective sigh from their assembled loved ones. This moment epitomized triumph over their past animosities, a true second chance rooted in shared beliefs and newfound understanding.

Applause erupted, drowning out the music as their loved ones rose to their feet in celebration. Ace's large, calloused, tattooed hand enveloped hers, squeezing gently, and together they walked down the aisle to the reception hall, smiling for the cameras. The reception was in full swing, the hall adorned with white lace and greenery.

Ace pulled her onto the dance floor for their first dance, his arms encircling her waist as they swayed to Brandon Lake's "Nothing New (I Do)." Melanie relaxed into his embrace, inhaling his woodsy scent, soothing her frayed nerves.

"Melanie," he whispered in her ear, his voice rough with emotion, "I'm doing this for us. I promise you won't regret this."

"I know," she replied, squeezing his hand. "I love you too, Ace."

As the ceremony gave way to celebration, and the reception hall buzzed with the chatter and laughter of guests. But the atmosphere shifted subtly when Rocco Moretti, a reminder of Ace's complicated past within the mafia, approached the newlyweds with a too-casual saunter and a smile that didn't quite reach his eyes.

"Congratulations, Mr. and Mrs. Andreas," Rocco said, extending his hand first to Ace, then to Melanie, who accepted it with a polite but firm grip.

"Rocco." Ace asked, his tone neutral, but Melanie could feel the tension coiling in his posture.

"This is certainty a beautiful occasion," Rocco replied, glancing around discreetly before continuing. "I just need a few minutes of your attention, Ace. A final loose end that needs tying up."

Ace's jaw tightened almost imperceptibly. Melanie knew that look—it meant he was on edge, ready to shield her from whatever threat loomed.

"Can it wait just a few more hours?" Melanie interjected, her voice calm despite the flutter of apprehension in her stomach.

"Darling, it's alright," Ace assured her, squeezing her hand gently. He turned back to Rocco, his gaze steely. "We'll handle it. But right now, my place is with my wife. We'll speak later."

Rocco nodded, though his eyes flickered with something unreadable before he retreated into the crowd. Melanie watched him go, feeling Ace's arm wrap around her protectively. She leaned into his embrace, focusing on the love that surrounded them, a bulwark against the remnants of a world they were leaving behind.

As the newlywed couple mingled among the sea of well-wishers, Melanie's fingers lightly brushed the hidden switch beneath the delicate lace of her gown. With a subtle click, too quiet for anyone but her to hear, she activated the wire. She cast a glance at Ace, who was already scanning the room with a vigilance that belied his relaxed smile.

"Everything okay?" she murmured, leaning closer to him under the pretense of affection.

"Always, when I'm with you," he replied, though his eyes remained watchful. He pulled her a little closer, his hand subtly shifting to rest against the small of her back—with each passing second, more assuredly over the concealed holster.

Melanie nodded, feeling the comforting weight of the wire's presence against her skin, a silent lookout amidst the revelry. She focused on Ace's warmth beside her, the steadiness in his touch, and the way his protective aura seemed to envelop her entirely.

"Remember, any sign of trouble, you get behind me," Ace whispered into her hair, his breath stirring the fine strands as they swayed gently to the music that filled the reception hall.

"Always my warrior clad in the full armor," she teased softly, hoping to lighten the tension that clung stubbornly between them despite the joyous occasion.

Ace's cocky grin flashed for a moment, the one she had fallen for all those years ago, now tempered with the gravity of his promise to protect her. "Someone's got to keep you safe," he said, his voice low and steady. "And I take that job very seriously."

"Especially today," she agreed, her voice imbued with an unspoken understanding of the stakes at play. They were a team—her grace balancing his strength, her faith intertwining with his burgeoning belief in redemption.

"Especially every day," Ace corrected, his gaze sweeping over the crowd once more, looking for any hint of danger lurking beneath the surface of their celebration.

"Forever and always," Melanie affirmed, her heart swelling with love for the man who stood by her side, ready to face whatever may come—with faith, love, and unwavering conviction.

Twenty-Six

A Chorus of Courage

Rocco Moretti slinked through the crowd, his eyes glinting with a predatory gleam as he approached Melanie and Ace. "Hello happy couple," he sneered, sidling up beside them with a swagger that belied his true intentions. "I'm tired of waiting, let get this over with."

Ace's jaw tightened, but his honey-colored eyes remained cool as he nodded to Melanie—a silent signal of their unspoken plan. "Why not?"

"Let's step over here," Rocco said, motioning toward a secluded corner of the opulent reception hall.

Melanie's pulse quickened; her subtle nod barely perceptible as she followed the men. She could feel the prickling sensation of danger, like static in the air, yet her demeanor remained calm and composed.

"Cut to the chase, Rocco," Ace demanded once they were out of earshot from the other guests. "What do you want?"

"Confidence suits you, Andreas," Rocco oozed, leaning against an intricately carved pillar. "But let's not forget who you used to run with. The Moretti family hasn't forgotten your... expertise."

"Is that so?" Ace's voice was laced with feigned curiosity. "I thought you just wanted to swipe the casino deal from underneath Bassito. I should have known there was something more. What exactly do the Moretti's have in mind?"

"Transport," Rocco replied, clearly enjoying the sense of control. "We need someone with your... discretion."

"Discretion doesn't come cheap," Ace countered smoothly, watching as Rocco's smugness faltered under the weight of implication.

"Money isn't an issue," Rocco snapped, his agitation beginning to show. "It's loyalty we're after."

"Here's a thought," Ace mused, his tone dangerously soft. "Why don't you confess all about these 'transport' activities? Might help me understand your needs better."

"Nice try," Rocco scoffed, but there was a crack in his veneer now, a split second where his ego hungered for recognition.

"Of course," Ace pressed, his words calculated, "the Moretti family wouldn't be moving anything... illicit, would they?"

"Ha! You think you're clever?" Rocco bristled, taking the bait. "We move what needs moving, and no one asks questions. And if they do—" He leaned in closer, his eyes darkening. "They end up regretting it."

"Sounds risky," Ace observed, a dangerous edge sharpening his words. "Risky for anyone involved—especially my wife."

Rocco's gaze snapped to Melanie, and she met it with an unwavering stare. "This type of business shouldn't concern a good Christian woman like yourself," he sneered.

"Indeed," Ace agreed, his protectiveness now masked by a facade of cold calculation. "Melanie, maybe you should reconsider your position. After all, Rocco here is offering us a chance at real power.

Rocco cut in, his voice low and menacing. "Listen to your man, doll. You think because he's wearing a white tux and made promises before God that he's out of the life? No one leaves my table without paying their dues."

The threat hung heavy in the air, and Melanie felt a shiver run down her spine despite knowing it was all part of the act. Her faith steeled her resolve, and she held Rocco's gaze, refusing to cower.

Ace squeezed her hand, “All we have to do is sign on the dotted line, take the money, and look the other way. Or else..."

"Or else what, Ace?" Melanie’s voice was steady, her big brown eyes revealing nothing of the fear that fluttered in her chest.

"Or else," Ace continued, meeting Rocco's challenge head-on, "we might find ourselves in a predicament we can't pray our way out of."

Rocco's laugh was dark and devoid of humor. "I knew you still had it in you, Andreas. I knew you hadn't gone completely soft with all this love and prayers nonsense. And that you'd come around."

"Let's just say," Ace whispered, his hand subtly shifting beneath his tuxedo jacket, close to the reassuring weight of his gun, "I'm full of surprises. But I'm curious, how are the, uh, imports doing these days?"

Rocco's lips curled into a smug smile. "Booming," he said, a little too loudly. "Once the new shipment comes through, we'll be set for years. You should've stuck around, Ace."

"New shipment?" Ace prompted, feigning interest.

"Top-quality stuff. And not just your average street walkers," Rocco boasted, oblivious to Melanie's subtle positioning, ensuring every word was captured by her wire.

Melanie watched the exchange, her heart caught between the hammering beats of fear and the unwavering trust she placed in the man she loved—the man who, despite the shadows of his past, stood ready to defend her with his life.

As the moment thickened with tension, Ace's instincts, honed from years in the shadows of his former life, flared to life. The subtle shift in the atmosphere was imperceptible to most, but to him, it screamed danger. His eyes darted around, catching the briefest glint of metal from a concealed balcony—a signal only someone with his past would discern.

"Melanie," he murmured, his voice low and urgent. Without waiting for her response, Ace acted, his body moving with a protective grace as he stepped in front of her, an unyielding shield against the unseen threat.

"What are you—" Melanie began, but her words were cut short by the sudden chaos that erupted.

Rocco, eyes wide with panic and desperation, fumbled inside his jacket. He drew out a gun, his hand shaking as he pointed it at Melanie with a snarl. "You think you can play me? You'll pay for this—"

"Rocco, don't!" Ace commanded, his own weapon now drawn in a swift, practiced motion. Time seemed to slow as he calculated the trajectory, his body coiling like a spring.

With a powerful shove, Ace thrust Melanie behind him, her gasp lost amidst the growing cacophony of alarmed whispers and shuffling feet. His finger tensed on the trigger, his aim never wavering from Rocco's contorted face.

"God forgive me," Ace whispered, and the sound of the gunshot was sharp, a definitive punctuation in the tense silence that had blanketed the room.

Melanie stumbled backward, her heart racing, her ears ringing. She watched, eyes wide, as Rocco staggered, the threat written across his features collapsing into confusion and fear.

Ace stood firm, the gun still raised, his stance that of a soldier ready to engage in battle for the sake of the one he loved. The intensity of his gaze held a fierce determination, a testament to his willingness to walk through fire for her.

"Are you okay?" he asked, turning to Melanie, his voice betraying none of the adrenaline that surely coursed through him. His concern was genuine, his role as her protector overriding all else.

Melanie nodded, unable to find her voice, too shaken to articulate the storm of emotions swirling within her. In that moment, the depth of Ace's love, his unwavering faith in their future, was as clear as the diamond on her finger—unbreakable, precious, and shining even in the shadow of danger.

The resounding echo of the gunshot reverberated off the windows and marble columns, an unholy symphony that jolted the guests from their matrimonial bliss into a frenzy. chairs emptied in a chaotic scramble, people clawing over each other, seeking refuge behind pillars and under the rows of tables, as if the carved wood could shield them from the violence that had erupted.

"Stay down!" Ace barked, scanning the room with sharp eyes, the muscle memory of his former life kicking in. His voice, though commanding, was a calm force amidst the screams and cries that filled the church.

"Melanie, behind me," he instructed, every fiber of his being ready to unleash hell should another threat present itself.

As the chaos unfolded, two figures cut through the panic with calculated precision. Jax, his dark hair a stark contrast against his pallid complexion, moved with the silent authority of a man who had faced danger more times than he cared to count. Tre's usually carefree expression was replaced with one of razor-sharp focus, his longer locks pushed back as he sprinted towards the commotion.

"Clear the exits!" Jax's voice boomed, authoritative and unyielding. Tre flanked him, his eyes darting around, cataloging faces, searching for signs of the impending ambush they'd been warned about.

"Undercover, move in!" came a shout, barely audible over the din. Agents, who had mingled among the guests disguised as distant relatives or old friends, emerged from their cover, badges glinting as they moved swiftly to secure the perimeter.

"Jax, left side!" Ace called out without turning, trusting his brother to cover the blind spot. Jax nodded, his movements synchronized with Ace's commands as he advanced, checking every shadowed corner.

"Tre, watch our six!" Ace continued, keeping his gun trained on Rocco, who lay motionless on the ground, a growing red stain beneath him serving as a grim reminder of the stakes they were facing.

"Got it, Ace!" Tre acknowledged, circling back to ensure no threat would catch them off-guard.

"Is everyone okay?" a voice trembled, the question almost lost in the pandemonium. It was Melanie, her bridal gown smeared with dust and debris, her voice a clear note of concern despite the terror that clung to the air.

"Everyone's safe because of you," Ace replied, not taking his gaze off the task at hand, but letting warmth seep into his tone for her benefit alone. "We've got this, love."

Melanie's heart hammered against her ribcage, the reverberations of the single gunshot still ringing in her ears. She stood motionless amidst the bedlam, her bridal train a stark contrast to the disarray around her. Ace pivoted toward her, his eyes locking onto hers with an intensity that cut through the commotion.

"Are you hurt?" he demanded, urgency lacing every syllable.

She shook her head, too stunned to find her voice. Amid the madness, it was Ace's unwavering gaze that anchored her, his presence a testament to the man he had become. The tattoos peeking from beneath his tuxedo sleeves no longer signified a past marred by violence but rather a canvas of redemption, each inked line a chapter in his journey towards grace.

"Stay behind me," he ordered, not as a command, but an impassioned plea wrapped in layers of concern.

The chaos around them began to ebb as Jax and Tre, along with the agents, secured the last of the rival members. Guests huddled together, their murmurs rising and falling like waves crashing upon the shore. Melanie glanced around, her eyes meeting those of her family and friends.

It was then she understood—the protective circle that Ace had drawn around her extended far beyond physical boundaries; it was woven into the very fabric of his soul.

Twenty-Seven

An Ode to New Beginnings

The faint wail of sirens approached the church, a discordant symphony to the evening's chaos. Blue and red lights flashed through the stained-glass windows, casting an otherworldly glow over the assembly of guests, who murmured in a mix of concern and relief.

"Looks like the cavalry has finally arrived," Ace said, his gaze never leaving Melanie, ensuring she remained shielded by his presence.

"Thank God," Melanie whispered, her voice steady despite the tremor that danced along her spine.

The hush that fell over the reception was profound, a collective breath held and then released in a surge of relief. As the last of the rival mafia members were escorted out in handcuffs, a ripple of applause burgeoned into an exultant wave. Friends and family rose from their pews, a sea of faces flushed with joy and wet with tears, converging around Ace and Melanie.

"God be praised," an aunt murmured, her hands lifted skyward. "They are protected by His grace!"

"Melanie, my girl!" Her mother's voice boomed as she pushed through the throng, her warm arms opening wide. Melanie met her halfway, nearly collapsing into her embrace. The strength of her hold conveyed the depth of worry, now dissipated.

"Thank you, Mom," she whispered, her voice muffled against her shoulder.

Ace stood a step away from the reunion, watching the display of affection with a protective gaze. The wrinkles and dust on his suit was a stark reminder of the peril they had faced, but the warmth in his eyes shone with something unbreakable.

"Come here, son." Her mother extended an arm to Ace, drawing him into the fold. It was more than an embrace; it was an acceptance, a blessing.

"Couldn't have done it without Him," Ace muttered, his voice rough with emotion.

"Nor without each other," Melanie's mother said, holding them both tight.

"Look at you two," beamed Melanie's aunt, holding them at arm's length. "Overcoming adversity like heroes in one of those novels you read."

Melanie laughed, a sound that danced merrily around the rafters of the church hall. "Except our story is real"

"Indeed," Ace agreed, sliding his arm around Melanie's waist tenderly. He looked down at her, his gaze softening. "You're my reality, Melanie. My beginning and end."

Tears shimmered in Melanie's eyes, but they were tears of happiness. She leaned her head against Ace's broad shoulder. "My rock," she murmured.

Ace kissed the top of her head, his action speaking volumes. "And you, my compass. You guide me home."

As the authorities filed into the holy sanctuary, their uniforms a stark contrast to the elegant attire of the wedding guests, Melanie's hand found its way to the small device concealed beneath her bridal gown. With a subtle movement, she unclasped the wire, the recording still humming with the evidence of Rocco Moretti's crimes.

"Detective Harris," she called out, her arm extending towards him, offering the wire as if it were an olive branch.

"Melanie Barnett, always one step ahead," he said with a nod, taking the device from her and immediately securing it in a plastic bag. His eyes flickered with respect. "This will go a long way in the prosecution."

As the danger receded and the night reclaimed its peace, the music of their hearts played on—a testament to the power of a love that conquered all and within the circle of their loved ones, Ace and Melanie stood, united not just by their past or the danger they had faced, but by the certainty of their future—guided by faith, strengthened by love.

"Let's make music together, forever," Ace said, echoing an earlier promise made beneath the soft glow of a candlelit gazebo.

"Forever," Melanie echoed, her heart secure in the harmony they had found.

Twenty-Eight

The Dawn of a New Day

The reception hall, bathed in the golden hue of a setting sun, was bustling with activity, but Ace's and Melanie's corner felt like the eye of a hurricane. Two FBI agents stood before them, their expressions serious as they leaned in over the table strewn with documents and audio recordings.

"Melanie has already given the recording from tonight to Detective Harris, but everything else we've gathered is here," Ace said, his voice steady despite the tumult around him. The tattoos on his forearms seemed to underscore his words, a testament to his past life—one he was now using to bring justice. His amber eyes flickered with a determination that matched the steel in Melanie's posture beside him.

Melanie, her big brown eyes focused and unwavering, nodded in agreement. She had organized every piece of evidence with meticulous care, her drive for perfection, not just in her dream wedding, but in all facets of life, now channeled into this moment of truth.

"Understood," Agent Barnes replied, flipping through the papers. "We'll take it from here."

"Make sure you do," Ace said, leaning back slightly, his protective nature evident even in how he placed himself subtly between Melanie and the agents. "We didn't risk everything for this to get botched."

"Your testimony could dismantle the entire Moretti operation," Agent Daniels added, her tone acknowledging the gravity of the situation. "You both are brave."

"Bravery comes easy when you have faith," Melanie said softly, her voice resonating with the strength of her convictions. "Faith in what's right, faith in each other."

As the agents began to collect the evidence, Ace observed every movement. He'd left the mafia behind, but the vigilance, the need to oversee everything—that remained. Melanie, however, exhaled a long-held breath, her shoulders relaxing as she watched years' worth of undercover work transfer from their hands to those of the law.

"Think of it, Ace," Melanie murmured, turning to him with a hint of relief breaking through her composed exterior.

"This... all of this means we're finally safe. That everyone can be safe from them."

Ace's response was a nod, the ghost of his cocky grin appearing for a moment. "Yeah, Mel, we did good."

The agents packed the last of the recordings, and with a final nod, they assured the couple once more, "We'll be in touch soon for the trial. For now, stay safe and lay low."

"Will do," Ace replied, his arm instinctively finding its way around Melanie's waist as they walked away from the table, the weight of their burden beginning to lift with each step toward the exit.

"Let's hope social media does its part too," Melanie added, thoughts of justice mingling with visions of her perfect church wedding, one step closer to being untainted by the shadows of Ace's past.

"Once this hits the news feeds, it's the beginning of the end for the Moretti's," Ace said confidently as they strolled through the crowd, unnoticed in the wake of the evening's earlier commotion.

"God willing," Melanie whispered, allowing herself to lean into Ace's side, her trust in him now fortified by their shared ordeal. Together, they crossed the threshold of the reception hall, leaving behind the chaos and stepping out into the promise of a future where love and faith reigned over fear and temptation.

Stepping out into the crisp evening air, Melanie clutched her phone, the screen alive with notifications. "Look at this, Ace," she said, her voice a mix of awe and disbelief.

Ace leaned over her shoulder, his protective presence both comforting and empowering as they read the latest news alert together: "Moretti Family Empire in Turmoil After FBI Raid."

"Wow, it's everywhere already," Ace muttered, his thumb scrolling through a cascade of social media posts. Tweets tagged #MorettiExposed and #MafiaTakedown were trending, each refresh bringing more shares and comments from a public hungry for justice.

"Listen to this one," Melanie said, clicking on a video of a newscaster detailing the evidence that had been uncovered. "The Moretti family's grip on the east coast's underground has been shaken tonight by a courageous couple who..."

"Courageous, huh?" Ace interrupted with a smirk, but Melanie could hear the pride in his voice.

She nudged him playfully. "Well, we did face them down together, didn't we?"

"True. But I couldn't have done it without you." Ace's eyes softened as he took Melanie's hand, squeezing it gently. "You're the brave one, Mel. Standing by me, even with... everything."

"Faith, Ace," she reminded him, her gaze steadfast. "I always believed there was good in you. And if God can forgive and give second chances, who am I to hold back?"

"Still, you've given up a lot for this—your dream wedding, placing your record on hold, the life on stage you wanted..." His voice trailed off as he looked away, his usual confidence waning at the thought of her sacrifices.

"Hey," Melanie said, tilting his chin to meet her eyes, "my dreams have changed. They're bigger now, it still includes being on the stage, but most importantly they include you. Besides, we've earned ourselves a fresh start, a real chance to build a life grounded in love, not fear."

"Mel, when I think about all that's happened—how we started, then got this second chance—it's a miracle." Ace pulled her into an embrace, the tension in his body easing as he held her. "And now, here we are, about to start a new chapter."

"Exactly," Melanie whispered, her head resting against his chest. "And speaking of new chapters, what do you say we get out of here, don't we have 4 hours before our charter for Italy leaves?"

"Absolutely," he chuckled, his laughter vibrating through her. "Nothing says 'new beginnings' like Italy. The food, the art, and amore."

"Amore," she echoed, her heart swelling with the promise of the days to come.

Ace and Melanie stepped out of the reception hall turned FBI's temporary command center, the cool evening air a balm to the clamor inside. The weight of the evidence they'd handed over still pressed on Ace's shoulders, though it was nothing compared to the weight that had lifted from his heart. They had done it; they had taken down Moretti and his goons, and now, as they walked through the dimly lit parking lot, the future beckoned.

"Mr. and Mrs. Andreas," came a voice smooth as aged whiskey. Vincent Basito emerged from the shadows near a sleek black limo parked at the curb. His tailored suit was impeccable, his silver hair slicked back with precision. He extended his hand first to Ace, then to Melanie, his eyes warm but assessing. "Congratulations are in order. You've both shown remarkable fortitude."

"Vincent." Ace clasped the older man's hand firmly, respect etched in his features. "Couldn't have done it without your help."

Melanie offered a tired but sincere smile, her relief palpable. "Thank you, Vincent. Your assistance meant everything. We were fighting a Goliath, and you helped us find our slingshot."

"Ah, but David's victory was always within him," Vincent said, nodding to Melanie's biblical reference. "You two merely uncovered what was already there—courage, faith, and an indomitable spirit."

"Still, we're grateful," Ace added, his protective nature flaring subtly as he kept Melanie close. "Especially knowing we can move forward without looking over our shoulders."

"Of course," Vincent assured, his gaze lingering on Ace for a moment before turning to the limo. "Speaking of moving forward, I've left a little something in the limo for you. Consider it a... token of my esteem for what you've accomplished."

Curiosity piqued, Ace's eyes sharpened. "A token?"

"Let's just say it's a gift for new beginnings," Vincent hinted, a wry twist to his lips. "And a reminder that the past never fully lets go—but it can be made to serve the future."

"Sounds ominous," Melanie teased lightly, though her eyes danced with intrigue.

"Think of it as a rite of passage," Vincent suggested cryptically.

Ace's chest hummed with anticipation, a mix of his old life's adrenaline and the fresh thrill of possibilities with Melanie. He was no stranger to valuable parting gifts, yet this felt different—more personal, more profound.

"Thank you, Vincent," Ace said, the words carrying the weight of their shared history. "For everything."

"Godspeed to both of you," Vincent replied, stepping back and giving them space to enter the limousine. "Enjoy Italy—and each other."

As Vincent disappeared into the night, Ace opened the limo door for Melanie, ensuring she was settled before sliding in beside her. The scent of leather and luxury enveloped them, a stark contrast to the gritty reality they'd just left behind.

"Ready to see what's waiting for us?" he asked, his voice low and eager.

"More than ready," Melanie responded, her hand finding his. "No matter what it is, we'll face it together."

"Always," Ace affirmed, feeling the truth of those words resonate deep within his soul. Together, they turned toward the mystery gift, the start of their new life just a heartbeat away.

The limousine glided through the darkened city streets, its interior bathed in a soft, ambient glow. Melanie's hand rested in Ace's, her fingers tracing circles over his knuckles in a silent symphony of comfort and solidarity. The atmosphere buzzed with anticipation, every nerve in Ace's body on edge as he contemplated what lay beneath the thick velveteen cloth shrouding their mysterious gift.

"Any guesses?" Melanie's voice was a melodic whisper, brushing against the tension that hung between them.

Ace shook his head, his honey-colored eyes alight with a concoction of excitement and trepidation. "With Vincent, it could be anything. But he knows us—knows me. It'll be something that marks a new beginning."

"Then let's not wait any longer," she said, her brown eyes reflecting the moonlight streaming through the tinted windows.

Together, they reached for the cloth, their fingers brushing against each other as they pulled it back with a flourish. The sight that greeted them stole the air from Ace's lungs—a briefcase lay open, revealing rows upon rows of meticulously arranged bonds, each one representing a slice of freedom from a past that had long sought to claim him.

"Twenty million dollars..." Melanie breathed out the sum in awe, her gaze flicking up to meet his. "For the sale of the casino?"

Ace nodded, the weight of the moment settling heavily on his shoulders. This was more than just money; it was a lifeline—a chance to build something untainted by the shadows of old sins. He lifted one of the bonds, feeling the crisp paper between his fingers, each one a testament to a future he had never dared to dream of.

But there was more.

Beneath the last row of bonds, nestled like a hidden treasure, lay a ring wrought from gleaming white gold, the Basito crest etched into its surface with undeniable craftsmanship. As he picked it up, he saw their names intertwined within the design—Ace & Melanie—a symbol of unity forged in the face of adversity.

"Vincent's protection... in the form of a ring." Ace's voice was thick with emotion, the significance of the gesture not lost on him. It wasn't just a ring; it was a vow, a promise carved in metal, ensuring that no harm would come to them as they journeyed forward hand in hand.

Melanie extended her finger, allowing Ace to slip the ring onto it, a perfect fit. "It's beautiful," she whispered, her eyes shimmering with unshed tears.

"More than that—it's a promise." Ace's words were fervent, filled with the understanding that the ring symbolized more than just the mafia's protection; it was a tangible representation of their commitment to overcome the darkness with the light of their love.

"From this day forward," Melanie murmured, leaning into Ace, her head resting against his shoulder. "In faith and love."

He wrapped his arm around her, pulling her close. "Against all odds, Mel. You and me."

Outside, the city passed by in a blur, but inside the limousine, time seemed to stand still. Here, in this sacred space, with bonds and ring as their witnesses, Ace and Melanie held each other, poised on the threshold of a life where love was their strongest defense and faith their guiding star.

Ace turned the ring between his fingers, its weight a comforting assurance of their safety. He glanced at the meticulously organized stack of bonds, then back into Melanie's warm brown eyes.

He pulled her into his embrace, the limo's plush interior fading into nothingness as he focused solely on the woman in his arms. "Italy," he said, a grin breaking across his face. "Our honeymoon. Just imagine the adventures waiting for us. I get to show you the family estate."

"Laughter, love, and a lifetime of memories to create," Melanie whispered against his chest.

"Against all odds," he murmured, pressing his lips to her forehead. "You and me, conquering the world side by side."

"Hand in hand," she echoed, tilting her head up to meet his gaze.

The limo slowed to a stop, and Ace could see the airport's lights flickering in the distance. Italy awaited them—a land of history, romance, and endless possibilities.

"Ready to conquer Italy?" he asked, the excitement in his voice palpable.

"Ready for our next great adventure," Melanie confirmed, her eyes sparkling with the promise of tomorrow.

They shared another kiss, brief but brimming with the intensity of their bond. As they pulled apart, the chauffeur opened the door, and the cool night air swept into the limo.

"Mr. and Mrs. Andreas," the chauffeur announced with a respectful nod, "your flight is prepared to board."

"Thank you," Ace replied, helping Melanie out of the vehicle with a protective hand at her back.

As they stepped onto the tarmac, Ace couldn't help but feel the weight of his former life lifting off his shoulders.

With each step toward their private jet, he felt lighter, freer. The roar of the engines signaled the beginning of their journey—a second chance carved from the trials of their past and the unwavering strength of their love.

"Here's to new beginnings," Melanie said, a radiant smile on her face.

"Here's to us," Ace agreed, his arm wrapped around her as they ascended the stairs to the jet that would whisk them away to their honeymoon and the rest of their lives. Together, they had overcome their enemies, mended their hearts, and now, under God's watchful eye, they were ready to soar.

Their lips met in a kiss that sealed their promises, a testament to the journey they had weathered and the bright horizon that beckoned. With faith as their guide and love as their shield, Ace and Melanie were ready to embark on a new chapter—one filled with hope, passion, and the courage to face whatever lay ahead. Together, they would write their own story, one where heart break was mended and a second chance bloomed into a lifetime of faith, love, and joy.

The Final Note

Epilogue

Melanie tilted her face up to the sun, letting its warmth seep into her skin. The melodic strumming of a guitar mingled with the gentle lap of waves against the shore. She opened her eyes to the vista of emerald hills rolling down to meet the sparkling blue of the Mediterranean Sea.

Strong arms wrapped around her expanding belly from behind as Ace pressed a kiss to her temple. "Beautiful view, isn't it?"

Melanie leaned back into her husband's solid frame, comforted by his protective presence. "I still can't believe we really did it. Our own villa in Positano."

"Nothing but the best for my wife and little one." Ace's voice rumbled low as his hands splayed across her pregnant stomach. Though they had only been back in Italy a few months, and it was if they had lived here their entire lives, the language and customs that were now part of their new life.

Melanie sighed contentedly, the horrors of their past now fading into memory as each day brought its own small joys - strolls through flower-filled piazzas, enjoying gelato by the seaside, quiet moments of prayer and devotion in their private chapel.

Their wedding had only been the beginning. With the Moretti's dismantled and Ace's mafia ties severed, they were finally free to live and love as they desired, bound only by their faith.

Melanie turned in Ace's arms to face him, tracing the contours of his handsome, bearded face. His honey-colored eyes gazed back at her with a devotion that made her heart skip.

"Ti amo," she whispered, the Italian phrase flowing naturally from her lips after months of practice.

Ace's eyes darkened with desire, and he captured her mouth in a searing kiss. She yielded to him, secure in the knowledge that this powerful, commanding man who had fought for her and protected her was now hers forever.

When they eventually broke apart, panting, Ace rested his forehead against hers. "And I love you, Melanie Andreas. Today, tomorrow, and every day after."

Melanie smiled, joy and anticipation welling up inside her. She placed a hand on her belly, feeling the light flutters of new life within.

"Our greatest adventure is just beginning," she said.

Ace grinned and kissed her softly once more. "That it is, my love. That it is."

Hand in hand, they turned back to take in the sweeping vista before them - the sea, the hills, their villa nestled among the cypress trees. The future stretched out, bright and full of promise, the last shadows of the past fading away in the Italian sunshine. Together, they had overcome all obstacles through resilience, faith and a love that bound them as strongly as the rings on their fingers. Now, they stood poised on the cusp of a new horizon, one they would continue exploring side by side, every step of the way.

The End

For a sneak peek into the future of Melanie & Ace read the extended epilogue on my member's only page by visiting https://authorabiegailrose.com/exclusives

Afterword

Did you know that I also wrote children's books under the pen name, Abbie Rose?

Come hang out with Abbie, as she teaches Duke his puppy manners. These books teach young children the importance of taking care of and training their dogs. Helping them to develop a trusting and safe relationship with their dog, under a parent's guidance, and in a fun way.

If you know a child who loves to read, click here to share the book. It's available on kindle or paperback.

About the Author

Abiegail Rose

Abiegail Rose is an author known for weaving tales of passion, heartache, and ultimate triumph in the world of love. With a gift for creating unforgettable characters and immersive stories, Abiegail's novels have captured the hearts of readers around the globe, earning her a loyal following.

Born with a love for storytelling, Abiegail began her writing journey at a young age, filling notebooks with tales of romance and adventure. Her unique ability to tap into the emotional depths of her characters has made her a standout voice in the romance genre, with each book exploring the complexities of love in its many forms.

In addition to her success as an author, Abiegail has a background in marketing, where she discovered the powerful parallels between crafting compelling love stories and creating engaging brand narratives. This realization inspired her to write *Love Lessons in Marketing: How Love Story Tropes Can Elevate Your Brand Strategy*, blending her two passions into a guide that helps brands connect with their audiences on a deeply emotional level.

When she's not writing, Abiegail enjoys traveling, indulging in classic romance novels, and exploring the latest trends in marketing and storytelling. She lives with her family in the Houston-Metro, where she continues to dream up new stories that inspire, entertain, and remind us all of the power of love.

Want to join her book club to be first in line for new releases?

Visit https://authorbiegailrose.com/

Follow her on Instagram @authorabiegailrose

Follow her on Goodreads

https://www.goodreads.com/abiegailrose

Follow her on Amazon

http://amazon.com/author/abiegailrose

Get a signed book: http://authorabiegailrose.com

Also by Abiegail Rose

Children's Books

Duke's Puppy Manners Series

The Lost Chronicles of Light Series

Sweet & Clean Romance

Ace's Heart: An Ex-Mafia, 2ndChance, Christian Romance

Love & Decay: A Zombpocalypse Romance (Kindle Vella)

Devotionals & Motivational

Let Your Light Shine: Rocking Your Purpose, Living Your Passion

Blessed Nourishment Vol. 1

49 Days of Self-Discovery

Prince, Not Required: Slaying your inner dragons, without dropping your crown!

Business

Love Lessons in Marketing: How Love Story Tropes Can Elevate Your Brand

Boss Babe Publishing: The Ultimate Self-Publishing Guide and Workbook

The Carter Effect: Hip-Hop 101

Boss Babe by Design

www.ingramcontent.com/pod-product-compliance
Lightning Source LLC
Chambersburg PA
CBHW070507300726
48975CB00007B/2360
* 9 7 9 8 8 8 9 4 0 8 3 6 9 *